Einstein's Secret

Irving Belateche

Laurel Canyon Press
Los Angeles

Library of Congress Control Number: 2014902307

ISBN 978-0-9840265-4-8

Edited by David Gatewood
www.lonetrout.com

Cover design by Karri Klawiter
www.artbykarri.com

Formatting by Polgarus Studio
www.polgarusstudio.com

Laurel Canyon Press
Los Angeles, California
www.LaurelCanyonPress.com

Also by Irving Belateche

Alien Abduction
Science Fiction Thriller

The Origin of Dracula
Supernatural Thriller

H2O
Science Fiction Thriller

The Disappeared
(A short story)
Supernatural Thriller

Under An Orange Sun, Some Days Are Blue
Autobiographical Novel

Prologue

In the late 1940s, Albert Einstein, the man who singlehandedly transformed the way we understand our universe, was well into his sixties, but his health was declining. He suffered from severe stomach pain and anemia.

In December 1948, his pain became so unbearable that he checked into Brooklyn Jewish Hospital in New York. There, doctors immediately rushed him into exploratory surgery and discovered that he'd had an aortic aneurism. To stop the aneurism from rupturing, they used a revolutionary technique. They wrapped his heart in cellophane.

That technique extended Einstein's life. But from that day on, the celebrated scientist knew he was living on borrowed time. To most of his acquaintances, he appeared to be fine. He continued to play the role of reluctant celebrity, a role he'd come to accept, lending his name and reputation to a few high-profile causes dear to his failing heart, and he continued to spend the bulk of his time working through thousands of equations, trying to discover the unified field theory, the theory that still eluded him.

But starting in late 1954, some of his close friends noticed that Einstein's demeanor had changed. The once buoyant professor was now more somber, as if something had started to weigh heavily on him, and they suspected that this something was more than his mortality.

Some of his friends suggested that it was his growing frustration at not yet having discovered the unified field theory. Others suggested it was something more pressing, perhaps a flaw he'd found in one of his established theories. And a few believed that he'd discovered something significant and that he wanted to share it with the world, but for some reason was reluctant to do so.

On the morning of April 13, 1955, seven years after doctors had wrapped Einstein's heart in cellophane, Einstein didn't leave for his office at the Institute for Advanced Studies at Princeton University. He was feeling sick, so he stayed home.

That afternoon, his long-time assistant, Ruth Meyer, heard him collapse in the bathroom. She called his doctor, who rushed over and gave him morphine. Einstein went to sleep, but it was clear to the doctor that Einstein's aneurysm had started to rupture.

The next day, a group of doctors arrived at Einstein's house and examined him. They recommended surgery and also told him that the aorta was probably too far gone to be salvaged. So Einstein refused the surgery, saying, "I want to go when I want. It is tasteless to prolong life artificially. I have done my share, it is time to go. I will do it elegantly."

*

If Einstein's wishes had been followed, I would've never discovered that the world's most famous scientist had a secret. He would've died at home and taken his secret with him.

But his wishes weren't followed.

The next morning, Ruth Meyer found him in severe pain and decided to call an ambulance. The ambulance arrived promptly, and Einstein was rushed to Princeton Hospital. At the hospital, he stabilized, and a couple of days later, on April 17, he said he felt well enough to write. He asked for paper and pencil, worked on some equations, then fell asleep.

Late that night, at 1:18 a.m., he awoke, spoke a few words in German, and died. Mrs. Ander, the nurse on duty at the time, didn't know German, so she didn't understand his last words.

History recorded that the last message from Einstein to the world, the last message that we could understand, was those pages he'd written, filled with equations. And I, like everyone else who'd studied Einstein's life, accepted history's judgment.

Until I came across a long-lost quote in a newspaper.

In the immediate aftermath of Einstein's death, many newspapers and magazines published articles about his last few days. He'd died at Princeton Hospital, so the local New Jersey papers also solicited quotes from the doctors and nurses who'd attended to the scientist.

Those papers all carried the same quote from Nurse Ander, the last person to see Einstein alive. They quoted her as saying that Einstein spoke a few words of German right before he passed away. Her quote was why this fact was so persistent in all that's been written about Einstein's death.

But one newspaper carried more of her quote.

The *Trenton Evening Times* also quoted her as saying that those words of German might've been the same words he'd written down a little earlier in the night. This quote was my gateway into Einstein's secret.

Nurse Ander was saying that Einstein hadn't written just equations on that final day, as history had recorded. He'd also written *words*. Words that I believed preserved a secret. Einstein had been hiding something from the world during the last year of his life, and he'd finally shared it on his deathbed. He'd confessed his secret rather than taking it with him to his grave, where it would have been forever buried.

And I was so sure of this, that I'd devoted the last twelve years of my life to uncovering that secret.

Chapter One

There is irrefutable evidence that the past existed, but everything else about the past is hearsay.

If anyone had asked me to sum up my theory of history, as I hurried across the campus of the University of Virginia, headed for the new faculty orientation, that's what I would've said. Almost any version of history can be supported by interpreting the facts in just the right way.

And that's exactly what I'd been doing for the previous twelve years. Taking facts, which were immutable, and bending them to fit my version of history. And my version of history was all about the great mystery I was trying to solve.

The way I saw it, you couldn't really get at the truth of past events without talking to the people involved. And even if you *could* talk to those people, how could you be sure they were telling the truth?

So while most men and women in their early thirties were fixated on laying the groundwork for their careers, I was treading water, postponing a career, fixated on a secret carried by a man who'd died more than sixty years earlier.

Luckily, this year I'd caught a break when it came to my career. Alex Turner, one of my former college classmates, was taking a sabbatical to work on a biography, and he'd recommended me to cover a couple of his classes. Even though he was the youngest professor in the department, he was already a rising star. His first book, a biography of Dwight D. Eisenhower, had made the *New York Times* bestseller list, so his recommendation had carried some weight.

Enough weight that I'd gotten the job and was now walking along the red brick walkways of this gorgeous campus, passing students lounging on green lawns, and hoping that this stint would put me back on track for a long-term teaching career. Thank you, Alex. Thank you for salvaging my teaching career from what the rest of my peers considered twelve years flushed down the toilet.

I was just about to step into Old Cabell Hall, the venue for the orientation meeting, when I heard a "hey" from behind me. I turned around and was greeted by a big, scruffy guy equipped with a backpack and a grin. "I'm Eddie Bellington, a friend of Alex's."

"Jacob Morgan," I said.

"How's McKenzie treating you so far?"

Benjamin McKenzie was the department chair, so I hesitated, trying to come up with a politically correct answer.

"Don't worry, I don't like him either," Eddie said.

"You're in the department?"

"*Was* in the department. I got my master's, but didn't make the cut for the Ph.D."

"Sorry."

"No worries. I found a more lucrative career."

"Want to let me in on it?"

"I collect stuff, or what other people call memorabilia." He adjusted his backpack and lost his grin. "You got a minute to talk?"

"Not right now."

"That orientation is bullshit. And McKenzie won't be in there if you're looking to make a good first impression."

It still seemed like a bad idea to miss my first official meeting. Plus this guy was coming on way too strong for my taste. "We can talk afterwards," I said.

"We can, but the sooner, the better."

"I'm sure it can wait."

"Haven't you waited long enough?"

That caught my attention.

"You know exactly what I'm talking about," he said.

It had to be Einstein's secret—and, if it was, he was right. I had waited long enough, and "waiting" was the right word, because the trail leading to Einstein's secret had reached a dead end a few years ago. My time was now spent rearranging the facts I'd already discovered, hoping that this would lead to a new theory. In other words, I was spending my time reinterpreting facts, rather than finding new ones.

The sad truth, one that I rarely admitted to myself and never admitted to anyone else, was how long ago it'd been since I'd come up with a significant lead. It had come right at the start of my quest. I'd stumbled onto it at a yard sale right before the second semester of my sophomore year.

I was looking for a lamp for my dorm room when I came across a box packed with old magazines. I rummaged through the magazines and came across a glossy tabloid called *Fame*, from 1955, with Albert Einstein on the cover. It caught my attention because I already had Nurse Ander's quote on my mind. I'd found her quote while doing research for a paper on Einstein's life for my History of Science course. The paper was done and handed in, so I didn't need to buy the magazine for more research.

But I bought it anyway. The coincidence of finding it made that inevitable.

That night, I read the article that went along with the glossy Einstein cover photo. It'd been written a month after Einstein's death, and the premise was that even though Einstein was a genius, he was also a regular Joe, like the rest of us. The article consisted of interviews with Einstein's friends. Tidbits on Einstein's love life, his daily routine, his favorite foods, et cetera. The interviews read like they'd been lifted from other publications.

But two sentences caught my attention. Like the rest of the article, they supposedly served as proof that Einstein was just a regular Joe.

To me, they proved something much more significant.

Like the rest of us, the sentences read, *Einstein also had secrets. And according to Henry Clavin, Einstein wrote one of those secrets down right before he died at Princeton Hospital.*

I was hooked. From the research I'd just done for my paper, I knew that Einstein had been writing down equations at the hospital. That's what history had recorded. *Except* for that one quote by Nurse Ander, a tiny inconsistency that stood alone in the *Trenton Evening Times.* Well, it no longer stood alone.

Henry Clavin confirmed that Einstein had written down more than equations on his deathbed. He'd written down words. And more than that, Clavin was claiming that Einstein had written down a secret.

Why had I been so eager to build a case around this? Because of one other fact I'd found while researching my paper on Einstein. Einstein had been worried about something during the last year of his life. Most historians assumed he was worried about dying before he discovered the unified field theory. But a few of

Einstein's friends thought Einstein had something critical he wanted to share with the world. Something he never did share.

Those who knew about my obsession with Einstein's secret thought that my quest was based on that fact and Nurse Ander's quote in a legitimate newspaper and a couple of other facts recorded by history. Facts that I still twisted through interpretation, but facts nonetheless. No one knew that the most critical fact, the one that validated my quest, came from a fifties tabloid magazine. If any of my colleagues had known that, I would've been subjected to more ridicule than I already was.

"I can wait a little longer," I told Eddie.

"It's not just up to you."

"I think it is." I was ready to end this and head into the orientation meeting.

"You won't think that anymore if you sit down and talk me."

"I have to go." I turned back to Old Cabell Hall. I was desperate for a new clue, but getting my career back on track had to be my top priority.

"Check this out," Eddie said.

I turned back around, and he reached into his backpack and pulled out an issue of *Fame*. *That* issue of *Fame*.

My mind went blank for a second and my chest tightened. The sight of a stranger holding up this obscure magazine was jarring. It was impossible that he knew this much about me. Not only did no one know the major role this gossip rag had played in my quest, but the magazine had gone out of business in 1955. The issue that Eddie was wielding, with its glossy cover photo of Einstein, had been its last, and, except for the issue that I had, I'd never found another copy.

"How'd you know about *Fame*?" I finally managed to croak out.

"I connected the dots."

That made me nervous. He couldn't possibly have meant he'd connected *all* the dots. "Which dots?" I said.

"All of them."

I skipped orientation, and he led me over to *Greenley's*, a coffee shop located in the heart of *the Corner*, a seven-block section of Charlottesville just across from campus, made up of bookstores, restaurants, and boutiques.

We each got coffees, no fancy frappes or lattes, just the straight stuff, my preference and apparently Eddie's, too, which made me think he might turn out to be okay.

He launched right in. "You think that Einstein was hiding something about one of his theories, right?"

"One dot down."

"You think that he found a flaw in one of his theories, but didn't want to cop to it."

"That's right."

"And finally, at the very last minute, he did the right thing."

"Yeah—But I don't have the evidence to really prove that. So no one believes me."

Eddie grinned. "Maybe they don't believe you because they know you're lying."

"What do you mean I'm lying?" I tried to sound insulted, but I wasn't. He *was* connecting all the dots.

"What you really believe is that Einstein discovered a new theory or some new scientific principle."

He was right. That was exactly what I believed. But I had never admitted that to anyone and I wasn't ready to admit it to him.

"But you tell people Einstein was ready to confess to an error in one of his earlier theories because it's easier for people to swallow that."

Now I was the one who was grinning.

"And you believe the reason Einstein didn't share this new theory with anyone was that he didn't have the mathematical proof he needed to convince anyone it was true. It was something he'd observed in reality or in one of his famous thought experiments, but couldn't prove."

I had to jump in. This was my baby after all. "It was something he'd observed. Not something from a thought experiment."

"You know that for sure?"

"It's just another dot."

"I think it's something he'd observed, too."

"So why didn't he just tell someone?" I had my own answer to that question, but I wanted to hear his.

"Well, that's the million-dollar question, isn't it?" He looked over to the other end of the coffee shop, and I followed his gaze and found Professor Benjamin McKenzie staring back at me.

I smiled at my new boss. He forced a smile back, then turned to the counter to wait for his coffee.

"Looks like you've been caught fraternizing with the enemy," Eddie said.

"Your exit from the program was that bad?"

"No, but my last words with McKenzie were." He looked over at McKenzie and we both watched the department chair grab his coffee and head out.

Eddie turned back to me. "I might be able to help you find out what Einstein wrote down that night."

"You're kidding, right?"

"You know I'm not."

"What have you got?"

"A clue of my own."

"What is it?

"If you help me, I'll share it with you."

Without knowing anything about the guy, it seemed crazy to commit to helping him. I wanted to talk to Alex first. After all, it must've been Alex who'd told him about my fixation on Einstein's secret. "Let me think about it."

"Okay," he said, and it was a confident "okay," as if he knew I couldn't resist pursuing any and all leads.

"So what kind of memorabilia do you collect?" I asked, hoping his answer might hint at what he'd found.

"Collect and sell. That's how the lucrative part works, thanks to Eddie's Emporium."

"Eddie's Emporium?"

"My eBay store: your destination for fifties memorabilia. Magazines, records, toys, sports programs, photos, movie posters, et cetera."

"Why do I have the feeling that I'd be most interested in the et cetera?"

"Because that's the best part of Eddie's Emporium. It's a collection of rare historical documents from the fifties. Letters and notes written by the famous and infamous. Public records that fell through the cracks of history. Any kind of documents that might have some historical value."

"So your history degree came in handy after all."

"Not as handy as the MS I'm working on in Computer Science. That's how I learned to mine the Internet for documents."

That was impressive and piqued my curiosity even more. What had he uncovered about Einstein's secret that I'd missed?

We talked a little more, mostly about the history department and how it was a political minefield, then he gave me his number and said to call him if I decided to take him up on his offer.

Chapter Two

I wanted to call Alex immediately, but restrained myself. This was a fresh start. A start where Einstein wasn't supposed to be a priority. So instead of punching Alex's number into my iPhone, I walked over to the Iliad Bookstore to pick up copies of my class handouts. Alex had recommended the Iliad, so I'd forwarded them PDFs of all my material before moving to Charlottesville.

Behind the counter, a woman in her late twenties was immersed in a book. Her short red hair swung down over one of her cheeks and even though she didn't glance up as I approached, I could still see that she was beautiful.

"Hi," I said.

She looked up and her hazel eyes completed the picture. "What can I help you with?"

"I'd like to pick up copies of my class handouts."

"Which class?"

"HIUS 5055."

Her jaw tightened, as if I'd made her angry. "So you're the lucky winner."

"Winner?"

"You got the job. You're Alex's college buddy."

She radiated hostility, and it took me a second to understand why. "You were up for the job?"

"Are you questioning my qualifications?"

"No—That's not what I meant. I—meant that Alex should have said something to me when he recommended the Iliad."

"Why? It's not his fault I didn't get the job."

She said it like it was *my* fault, and I was at a loss for words.

She got up and started toward the back of the store. "Now that the cat's out of the bag, I'll get your class materials."

I wanted to smooth this over, and tried to come up with something to say. I hadn't thought of anything by the time she returned.

She plopped a box loaded with my handouts down on the counter.

"Did you go to grad school here?" I said. It was the best I could do.

"Is that so hard for you to believe?" She rang up my tab. "Seventy-four fifty."

I handed her my credit card. "Do you want me to resign?"

She almost cracked a smile. "Won't do much good. I'm sure I'm not next in line."

"But classes start in two days and you're available."

She handed me back my credit card. "If Alex recommended you, you must have something going for you."

"Or I know a secret about his sordid past."

"Are we talking about the same Alex?"

"So you know him that well, huh?"

"Mr. Squeaky Clean," she said. "No wonder he wrote a bestseller, huh? He never left his study carrel during grad school, and he kept it as a professor."

"He was the same in college. He spent every waking minute either studying, researching, or reading."

"Were you the same way? Is that how you got the appointment?"

"Nope. I got lucky."

It looked like she was about to break into that smile, but the phone rang, interrupting what might have been.

She answered the phone. "The Iliad. This is Laura." She listened for a few seconds, then said, "I'll check," and turned to her computer terminal.

I grabbed the box, weighed whether to say more, then headed out. At least I'd ended the conversation on a good note, and picked up her name—*Laura*—as a bonus prize.

"Hey! You forgot your receipt," she said. "The department is a stickler."

I walked back to the counter and she handed me the receipt.

"I'm sorry you didn't get the job," I said.

"Yeah, me too. You know how it is out there for PhDs. I'd kill for that job."

"I'll watch my back."

The full smile finally appeared. "Good plan," she said, then picked up the phone and began to list the various editions of *The Stranger* to the caller on the other end.

As I headed out, I couldn't help but look back over my shoulder. She glanced up at me, and before she looked back down at her computer terminal, I thought I glimpsed approval in her hazel eyes.

*

During the drive back to my apartment, she was on my mind. And I tried to keep her on my mind when I walked into my apartment. Otherwise, I'd go back to thinking about Eddie and Einstein.

I couldn't do it. Einstein beckoned.

I called Alex, who was in New York, conducting interviews for his next biography.

"Why are you asking me about Eddie Bellington?" he asked.

"He said he knows something about Einstein's secret."

"Jesus Christ! You said you were giving that a rest."

"I am. Just fill me in on Eddie."

"My advice is to focus on UVA this year. Eddie will always be there. He isn't going anywhere."

"You don't actually think he found something, do you?"

"Listen, McKenzie hates him, and you don't want McKenzie thinking that you're somehow mixed up with him."

"Then you're not going to like this—I bungled that already."

"What? How's that even possible? You've only been there a couple of days."

"Just bad luck. McKenzie saw me at a coffee shop with him."

"Doesn't sound like bad luck. The guy roped you into talking to him."

"Will you at least tell me his story?"

I heard an exasperated sigh.

"Here's the synopsis. He was in the program for years, a brilliant researcher, but not so hot on coherent synthesis. McKenzie gave him one extension, but wouldn't approve another one. Eddie's side business didn't help his cause either."

"The fifties memorabilia."

"That part was kosher. It was the documents and records. The things with historical value."

"He thinks Eddie's a commercial archeologist."

"And he's right."

So McKenzie spotting me with Eddie was worse than I'd thought. Commercial archeologists were disdained by academia. They were considered crass treasure hunters who sold their finds to the highest bidder rather than donating them to research institutions or museums.

"But what McKenzie didn't like the most about that," Alex said, "was that Eddie was good at it. He helped me out with my research a couple of times when I first got to Charlottesville, so I learned the hard way."

"McKenzie put you in the doghouse?"

"I got away from Eddie in the nick of time. Barely. You need to avoid the guy."

"Alex, was it worth it?"

"What do you mean?"

"His research. Did it help you?"

Alex hesitated before answering, and that was all I needed to know. Eddie's research had been worth it, and that meant he might've found a clue about Einstein's secret.

"He's a nut," Alex said, but it was too late. His hesitation had been the true answer. "You're not there for Einstein. You're there to make up for lost time. Secure your position with the department and try to turn it into a longer gig. We talked about that. That's the whole point. Don't get involved with this guy."

"You're right," I said, but thought, *one conversation with the guy isn't going to derail my year.*

We exchanged goodbyes, and just as I was about to call Eddie, my phone rang. It was the history department's administrative assistant. "Professor McKenzie would like to set up a meeting with you in the morning," she said. "Are you available at ten?"

My first thought was paranoid and reactionary. Alex's warning had been right. Eddie was trouble, and the trouble had already started. McKenzie was meting out punishment.

I told the assistant I'd be there, then tried to come up with a less paranoid scenario. McKenzie just wanted to ask me to serve on a faculty committee where he was shorthanded. Still, the pending meeting put me on notice, and my call to Eddie was put on hold. Hopefully permanently, but I couldn't promise myself that.

I didn't have much planned for the rest of the day. Grocery shopping and my daily Internet search for new information about Einstein's last year. I considered adding a trip to the Iliad to ask Laura out, but that'd be coming on too strong, too soon.

The prep for my classes was done. One class was an American history survey course, similar to another class I'd taught when I'd been lucky enough to land an adjunct position right out of graduate school. The other was a history of science course, the type of course I would've loved to have taught year in and year out.

I did my Internet search first. For the last six years this was a daily routine, and every once in a great while, some new fact would turn up or another fact would get confirmed. But usually months would go by with nothing.

And "new fact" was a relative term. It usually meant a new secondary or tertiary source rehashing an old fact. Rarely did I find a real new fact. The reality was that not every historical document and record was on the Internet. Plenty of material hadn't been digitized, uploaded, or indexed. And that meant new facts were hard to come by.

I spent an hour online, then went to the grocery store. I loaded my cart with enough food for two weeks' worth of dinners. In the checkout line, my iPhone buzzed. It was a text from Eddie.

I need to see you tonight, before the clue is gone forever.

As I stared at the text and contemplated my next move, the grocery story clerk finished scanning my items. "Go ahead and swipe your card," he said.

As I did, I thought about Alex's warning. He'd called Eddie a nut, which was why I feared getting involved with him. Not because I, too, thought he was a nut. But because I saw that Eddie was a version of me. An academician whose love of research and theorizing had led him down the path to ruin.

And, of the two of us, I was worse. I was the bigger nut. A crackpot. My energy was channeled into an obscure pursuit that no one validated, while Eddie's was channeled into the far more lucrative fields of fifties memorabilia and commercial archeology.

I wheeled my grocery cart to my car and let this sink in. Did I view Eddie as some kind of buffoon or freak? Or failure?

I didn't.

And actually, I felt just the opposite. From what Alex had said about him and from talking to him, I could tell he was a smart guy, accomplished in his own right.

I texted him back. *Where do you want to meet?*

Chapter Three

Two hours later, I met Eddie at the Corner and we headed to the Caves.

"The Caves are a series of secret carrels under the Lawn," he said, as we walked across campus. "The Lawn is the original part of UVA. All its buildings were built in the eighteen twenties and designed by Mr. UVA himself, Thomas Jefferson."

We walked past the Rotunda.

"A hundred years later, in the nineteen twenties, the University built new underground tunnels, the ones that carried steam, water, and power. And they also closed down some of the old ones, including the ones under the Lawn.

"A decade later, a graduate student broke into those tunnels and he and his buddies spent the next year building study carrels down there. Then he turned the privilege of using the carrels into one of UVA's secret societies. The Cabal. And like most of the school's secret societies, it's not so secret."

"Are you in the Cabal?"

"Yep."

"You don't seem like the 'joiner' type."

"I'm not. But this was too cool to pass up. Plus I didn't have to do anything. There's no rush or crap like that. You're invited in by existing members. You've got to be a graduate student and you get judged by your academic research. That's it."

"So it's a kind of nerd secret society."

"Of the highest order."

"Congrats, then."

"I got in before my dustup with McKenzie. For a research paper I did on fifties genre films and the American dream."

That slowed my pace. Films were my dad's big thing, but I didn't want to think about my dad. So I didn't. "How did you keep your carrel after leaving the history department?"

"I'm doing pretty well with research in comp. sci., too."

I wasn't surprised, and that made me even more curious about the clue he had.

We entered Grace Hall. The entrance to the Caves was in the basement. "I met Alex because of the Caves," Eddie said. "He was invited to join in his third year and he lobbied to keep his carrel after he graduated."

"And the Cabal said 'yes' because they liked having a famous professor in their ranks."

"Yep. But what I don't get is why Alex needs a carrel anymore. The cash from being a full professor and from his biography is enough to buy him some privacy above ground."

We took the stairs down to the basement and walked through a corridor lined with storage cages. At the end of the corridor was another staircase leading down to a small sub-basement. The sub-basement looked straight out of the 1800s, when the University was founded. Its stone walls and floor must've been part of the original Grace Hall.

The tiny space was empty except for a trap door built into the floor. The door was made of dark oak like something out of a gothic horror movie, but embedded in the oak was a modern electronic keypad.

Eddie punched numbers into the keypad, and I heard a loud click. He then grabbed an iron ring that folded up from the door, pulled the door open, and we climbed down into the Caves using slots carved into the wall.

I was now standing in a narrow tunnel. It was lit, very dimly, by battery-powered lights that ran into the shadowy distance.

Eddie took the lead, navigating down the tunnel, then another, and another. Old, dead pipes ran above us, and stone walls ran alongside. We passed very few doors and, of those, only a few were open, revealing students hunched over computers or books.

"There aren't that many carrels," I said.

"They're spread out for maximum privacy, and there's over a dozen tunnels down here."

"Is there Internet down here?"

"Nope. That's one of the Caves' best features. You come down here to work, not to surf. There's no cell phone reception down here either."

"No wonder Alex likes it."

We hiked deeper into the labyrinth of old tunnels, so deep that I would never have been able to find my way out on my own. "The University can't be on board with students coming down here."

"It's considered trespassing and a Class One Misdemeanor." Eddie looked over his shoulder and saw the unease on my face. He grinned. "I mean technically, but they turn a blind eye to members of the Cabal coming down here. The Caves is a longstanding tradition, and UVA is all about tradition."

We finally arrived at Eddie's study carrel. He unlocked the door, and I stepped into an eight-by-eight room, furnished with a desk and three bookshelves, surrounded by the Caves' now-familiar stone walls. Plastic storage boxes, stacked three high, took up the rest of the space.

"Have a seat," he said, and I sat down in the only chair available. The one behind his desk. Eddie opened one of the plastic storage boxes. "Henry Clavin—How much do you know about him?"

"More than anyone does. Not that there's much to know." After I'd read Clavin's quote about Einstein in *Fame*, I'd dedicated a couple of years to tracking down everything I could about the man.

Eddie pulled a file out of the box. "Tell me what you *do* know."

No harm in that. "Einstein met him in Princeton in the fifties. I don't know how he met him. My best guess is that it was on one of those long walks he was famous for taking. That's when he'd talk to the locals not affiliated with the University. And Clavin wasn't part of the University. At least, I was never able to find a link. He was born in Maryland. I found a public record of that. But I don't know when he moved to Princeton or where he lived when he was there."

"Anything else?"

"I'm sure he wasn't one of Einstein's highfalutin friends because he didn't leave much of a trail in the annals of history."

"That's it?"

That wasn't it. I didn't tell him the most intriguing thing I knew. But I did give him one more thing. "The last trace Clavin left was in 1970. He died in a car accident."

"He's not dead."

What? That was crazy talk. I leaned back in my chair, with one thought going through my head. Alex's warning. *He's a nut.* My research skills weren't the best, but when it came to Henry Clavin, they were good enough to confirm that the man was, indeed, dead.

"I'm sure you double-, triple-, and quadruple-checked your sources," Eddie said. "So I don't expect you to just take my word for it."

"I don't." Henry Clavin had died in a car accident in 1970. It was documented not only in a newspaper account of the accident, but also in an obituary, a death certificate, and a funeral announcement.

"Two days ago, I found out he was still alive," Eddie said. He handed me a printout. "This is a newsletter from a place called 'Inn on the Boulevard.' It's an assisted living facility in Rockville, Maryland."

My eyes went to a headline halfway down the page: *Long-Time Resident Talks About Friendship With Einstein.* In the first paragraph was the name of the long-time resident, *Henry Clavin.* In one quick gulp, I read the four-paragraph story. Clavin was quoted as saying that Einstein was both brilliant and friendly and liked to talk about politics. There wasn't much more to the story than that.

I immediately started to calculate Clavin's age. I remembered that he'd been forty when Einstein died, so if he were still alive, he'd be ninety-eight.

But he wasn't ninety-eight. He died in that car accident in 1970.

"How'd you find this?" I said.

"Every couple of weeks, I run a search program on unsecured servers in D.C. and its suburbs. The federal government is so huge that there's a hell of lot of information passing through those networks. I search for keywords associated with two things. Fifties memorabilia or documents dealing with historical figures or events. I find a lot of stuff that way."

"You mean you were looking for Clavin."

"No—that was a total fluke. My search flagged the newsletter because there's an article in there about another resident. He collects movie posters from the nineteen fifties. And the only reason that newsletter was on a government server was that a Commerce Department employee has her mom in that retirement community and she gets their newsletter in her email."

I looked back down at the newsletter and saw the headline at the bottom of the page, *A Valuable Hobby*. Skimming through the article told me that resident Milt Taylor had collected movie posters as a teen, kept them all, and now believed they were worth thousands.

"I want you to go up there and talk to Clavin," Eddie said.

I have to focus on UVA and on a real career was my immediate reaction. *This is a fresh start.*

But Einstein beckoned. "Why are you into this?" I said.

"I wasn't until I found that newsletter. I've dealt in some Einstein memorabilia, nothing of any real value. Just junk like that *Fame* magazine. That's how I knew about Clavin in the first place. But here's the weird thing. I stumbled onto that newsletter two days ago, right when the one person who'd be most interested in Clavin moved to Charlottesville—you."

That had been at the back of my mind since he'd shown me the newsletter. This was one of those coincidences that was so big, you wanted to believe there was a grand synchronicity to life.

And I'd soon learn that there was. Not to all lives, but to lives that were entangled in a special kind of vortex. A vortex that, at that moment in the Caves, I could never have imagined existed.

"Why don't you go it alone?" I said. "You found the smoking gun."

"I *will* go it alone if you don't want to help. But this is all about Einstein's secret, and you've got the home field advantage. If I talk to Clavin, maybe I get the right answers, maybe I don't. I don't even know the right questions. But if you're there, you'll make the right connections. If you're there, that little newsletter could lead to a discovery that changes everything we know about Einstein's work."

The game was over. Eddie had won. "I can't go right away," I said. "I have to meet with McKenzie in the morning. Then Tuesday, I start classes."

"It can't wait."

"Why not?"

"Clavin's in the hospital with an infection. A bad one. At ninety-eight years old, he might not last another hour, much less another day. That's why I texted you; this clue might be gone forever."

I took a deep breath. I didn't want to confess that my lack of urgency stemmed from wanting to salvage my career. "The odds that Clavin knows what Einstein wrote on those pages are slim. And even if he did know at one time, it was a long time ago, and the odds that he still remembers are even slimmer."

But under any other circumstances, those odds would have been more than good enough for me.

Eddie stared at me for a few seconds, giving me a look that said, *Come on, really, you're not curious?*

I handed the newsletter back to him, and he put it in the file.

"I'm driving up there to talk him tomorrow," he said. "I think you're making a mistake by not coming with me."

*

As we snaked through the tunnels on our way out of the Caves, an obvious question came to me. "Why'd you bring me down here to show me the newsletter?"

"I keep my valuable stuff down here."

That didn't make any sense. "It was a printout. You can print out a million copies."

"I can't explain that to you without filling you in on a couple of other things."

"Go ahead—I'm all ears."

"I was going to explain it all on our trip to Rockville."

"Why not now?

"It's going to take time."

"Okay, how about answering this question. Clavin's death was well documented. Was it faked?"

"That's part of what I wanted to explain on our trip."

This was getting annoying. "You're not talking conspiracy, are you?" Asking him that was a not-so-subtle insult. As historians, we both knew that the vast majority of conspiracies were complete perversions of history. Conspiracies were the domain of kooks who created them by taking known facts and adding their own.

"Please. Have more faith in me than that," he said.

I didn't press him anymore, which was a good thing. Not that he would've explained anything about was going on right then anyway. If he had, it would've made a conspiracy look like a rational explanation by comparison, *and* it would've made me run as far away from him as possible.

We climbed out of the Caves and exited Grace Hall. I expected him to push me to go Rockville one last time, but he didn't. Of course, he didn't have to. It was the only thing on my mind.

Chapter Four

We parted ways, and I walked across the Lawn, planning to drive back to my apartment. After my little tête-à-tête with Eddie, there was no doubt about how I was going to spend the rest of the evening and probably a good chunk of the night. I'd be digging through my notes on Henry Clavin and searching online for anything that I'd missed.

Like the fact that he was still alive.

Students were strolling along the brick walkways, laughing, chatting, and enjoying the evening breeze. Charlottesville was always hot and muggy in late August, so any breeze, even a warm one like this evening's, was welcome.

So welcome, in fact, that it inspired me to try and change my plans for the night. I veered south, toward the Iliad, ready to ask Laura out. It would still be coming on too strong, too soon, but it was better than succumbing to the lure of Einstein's secret.

*

She was behind the counter, reading, but this time she looked up when I walked in and she definitely looked surprised to see me. "Was there something wrong with your order?" she said.

"Nah. I was just wondering if I you'd like to grab dinner when your shift is over? You know, to let me make up for taking the job from you."

"It's going to take dinner every night, plus subsidizing my rent, to make up for that."

"Can't do that. Don't get paid enough."

"Yeah, that's the worst part. I'd kill for a job that pays less than working here."

"I hear that teachers in Finland get paid top dollar."

"Thanks for the tip."

"No problem. Dinner will be packed with helpful tips like that."

"That sounds irresistible." She brushed her hair away from her eyes. "My shift ends at eight."

"Great, I'll swing by then."

"Just meet me at Jackson Hill at nine. You can join me for my hike."

"...Okay. You hike at night?"

"You catch on quick."

I laughed. "Where's Jackson Hill?"

"Google it. And bring sandwiches for the dinner part."

I liked this woman even more this time than the first time I'd met her. And I had liked her a lot that first time.

*

When I got to Jackson Hill, Laura was already there. She was wielding a flashlight and a blanket, waiting by her car in the small, unpaved parking lot.

I stepped out of my car, and she pointed her flashlight at the bag I was holding. "What'd you get?" she asked.

"A turkey and cheese. A veggie. And a tuna salad."

"You covered all the bases."

"To make sure, I also got a slice of chocolate cake."

"Kind of defeats the purpose of a hike."

"Yeah, but in a good way."

She smiled, then walked over to the head of the trail. "The view from the top is unbelievable."

"But it's night."

We started up the trail. "That's the point," she said. "The top of the hill overlooks Sherman Valley, which hasn't been developed yet. So there's no light pollution. You can see the night sky and the stars and what darkness really looks like."

"You like the dark?"

"I like the dark of night."

"You're not secretly a vampire."

"You'll see when we get up there."

"You mean, if you're a vampire?"

She looked over her shoulder at me, and flashed another smile. "See why I like the view."

We fell into silence as we settled into a steady pace. The air was cool and invigorating. She followed the trail like an experienced hiker, so I just followed close behind her, in her footsteps.

After a little more than an hour, we made it to the top: a small plateau that overlooked a dark valley. And just as she'd said, the dearth of lights from the valley below highlighted the open sky above, dark and speckled with bright golden stars. It *was* a striking view.

She unfolded the blanket, and I pulled the sandwiches out from my bag. I also pulled out a bottle of wine and cups.

"I brought a bottle of water, if you don't like wine."

"Who doesn't like wine?"

We sat down.

"This beats a restaurant on the Corner," she said.

"Yeah…"

"But it's a bit romantic for a casual get-together?"

I grinned.

"I can make it less romantic," she said. "I'm thinking of going to law school next fall."

"And you invited me up here to talk you out of it."

"Yep."

"Guess what? I think it's a good idea."

"So does everyone else."

"But you're still not convinced."

"You know how some people feel that there's something they have to do?"

Like hunt down Einstein's secret at all costs. "Yeah."

"I'm one of those people. I've wanted to teach since I was a kid, and I'm good at it."

"What about teaching high school?"

"It's an option. I'm a sub already."

She took the veggie and I took the turkey and cheese. Then I poured us each a cup of wine.

"My mom was a high-school history teacher," she said. "And my dad was a math teacher."

"So it runs in the family." I was hoping she wouldn't ask about my family. "What do they think of law school?"

"I'm too old to worry about what they think."

"So they're against it."

"I wish they were, but they think it's a great idea. They'd love me to be a teacher, but they think it's impossible to get a university appointment, and they think high-school teaching is a much harder life than it used to be."

"You'd have to leave Charlottesville to go to law school, and my bet is you love it here. I mean look at this view."

"That's just it. I wouldn't have to leave."

"UVA is a tough law school to get into."

"Are you doubting my qualifications, again?"

"I gotta stop doing that."

"Yeah, especially because I already got accepted."

"Congratulations." That was impressive, but I didn't want to add that, or she'd think I was doubting her qualifications once again.

"I deferred for this year because I was hoping to get your job," she said.

"So we're back to that."

"The one thing you wanted to avoid."

"Yeah." Though I was glad we'd avoided talking about my family.

"So how'd you get into the history of science?"

I looked up to the sky and pointed to a spot just above the horizon. "That's Ursa Major. The great bear. And that over there, that's Orion."

"It started with astronomy," she said.

"You catch on quick."

She grinned.

"From astronomy, I went on to chemistry and physics, but it turned out that I was good at the general principles, but not so good when it came to the nitty-gritty."

"So history gave you a way in, without having to do the nitty-gritty."

"As my dad used to say, where there's a will, there's a way."

"Tell me about your dad."

So, I had brought up the one thing I didn't want to talk about. The attraction I felt toward her must've caused me to slip up, and my instinct was to pull back before it was too late. But Laura's hazel eyes, sincere and direct, drew me further in.

"He died when I was really young," I said. "I was five, so I didn't really know him."

There was an awkward silence, and I saw a tear form in her eyes. "I'm so sorry, Jacob." She turned away to wipe the tear, then looked back.

"No big deal." I pasted on a self-conscious smile. "It was a long time ago."

So long ago that I had just one memory of my dad. We were in a movie theater and he was glued to the big screen up front. I looked up at him and saw that he was bathed in blue light. He laughed at some hijinks unfolding up on the screen, then looked down at me.

His eyes were the bluest eyes I'd ever seen, then and since. They were alive with joy, a true incarnation of happiness. I laughed with him, so I could be part of his happiness, and not because of anything going on in the film. I don't remember the film.

I learned later that my dad had loved movies and had started taking me to see them when I was three. Once I knew that, I replayed that memory of him, the only one I had, over and over again. My dad laughing in a dark movie theater with me by his side, sharing in his joy. I treasured that memory as if it were a classic film itself.

To end that train of thought, I focused back on Laura. She was looking down at the valley, sipping her wine, taking her cue from me about when to start up the conversation again.

But when I looked down at the valley, the vast darkness of the night engulfed me with a feeling of absolute loneliness. The same loneliness I'd felt during my freshman year of college. All my new friends were looking forward to going home for the Thanksgiving break, but I wasn't. I had no home to go back to. My mom had died right before I'd left for college. She'd been everything to me.

"How long ago did you graduate from the program?" I finally said.

"Five years ago," Laura answered. "And I lucked out when I finished. I got a one-year appointment at William & Mary. But they had nothing the next year. Then I was stupid. Or arrogant. I had an offer at a community college in Miami, but I didn't take it. I held out for a better job that never came."

I appreciated Laura's long answer. It was just what I needed.

"Let me guess, the person who took that job is still there," I said.

"Yep. And from what I know about him through a friend at Florida State, he loves it."

"Well, nothing you can do about it now."

"Except go to law school."

"The perfect alternative."

"You found another alternative."

"I fell into it. A few years ago, I saw an opening for a job at USC. They'd gotten a National Science Foundation grant and they were looking for people to administer it. I applied and got the job."

"What's the job?"

"Developing science curriculums for high schools."

"Kind of up your alley."

"Yeah. I liked it just enough to make me lazy. I stopped hunting down every single teaching gig."

"Well, it doesn't take much to stop the hunt when you feel you're hitting your head against a brick wall." She stood up. "Let me show you what I was working on when I should've been applying to every opening in the country."

*

She took me down another trail, on the east side of the hill, and though I didn't know it yet, she was about to show me the real reason she loved Jackson Hill. "Back in the fifties, this entire area was real wilderness," she said. "There weren't any hiking trails, and even hunters didn't come up this way."

After we'd gone about three hundred yards, the trail leveled off, and the thick patch of forest gave way to a tiny clearing and a small log cabin.

"Welcome to Gray's Cabin," she said, and opened the cabin door. "After I moved back from Williamsburg, this is one of the projects that kept me busy. You know, while I was holding out for that perfect job."

She stepped inside and flicked on a light, revealing a windowless cabin that had the clean, neat look of a museum exhibit, which it basically was.

At the far end of the cabin was a small cot, covered with a clear, protective plastic sheet. Along another wall ran a counter displaying metal plates, a metal pot, an iron skillet, and utensils. Catty-corner to the counter was a black, wood-burning stove. And along the opposite wall, there was a glass display case containing books.

"Corbin Gray built this cabin," Laura said. "He was a UVA student in the fifties who wanted to live in the real wilderness for one year. No modern conveniences allowed. So he spent one year building this and the next year living in it."

"Was he a beatnik?"

"He was an transcendentalist."

"Emerson and Thoreau," I said, trying to remember what else I remembered about transcendentalism.

"Exactly. He was ready to commune with nature, so he came up here for a year and lived by two rules. He wouldn't leave, and he'd only eat what he could hunt, grow, or pick."

"Wait—I'm missing something. How did this keep *you* busy?"

"I restored the cabin and made it a destination spot. It's not exactly Disneyland, but, believe it or not, quite a few people drop by to check it out."

She walked over to the display case and flipped open what must've been a guest registry on top of it. "Twenty-five people last week. Not a bad week, considering how oppressively hot it was. During the fall and spring, it's about a hundred a week."

I moved over to the case. Inside were the works of Thoreau, Emerson, Fuller, Whitman, and other transcendentalists.

She closed the registry. "In my third year in the doctoral program, I wrote a journal article on transcendentalism. While I was researching it, I found out about Corbin and this cabin. His adventure had fallen through the cracks of history."

At the end of the display case, I saw something that startled me. It didn't fit with the theme of the cabin, but that wasn't why it startled me. It startled me because it was another strange coincidence. *Two coincidences.*

It was an issue of *Life* magazine from 1955, the year of Einstein's secret, and on its cover was a photo of Dwight D. Eisenhower, the subject of Alex's bestselling biography.

I didn't know it, but synchronicity was at work. I was far from understanding what these coincidences meant, but I was already entangled in their vortex. "How is that *Life* magazine connected to Corbin Gray?" There was definitely too much concern in my voice.

"Take a closer look."

I did, and saw that in the lower corner was a photo of a scraggly mountain man with the caption: *Back to Nature.* So that, at least, was a partial explanation for the coincidences.

"That's Corbin?" I said.

"Yep."

"And what did he discover up here?"

"That there was a timeless quality to life. And that you could only get to it if you lived outside of society."

"Outside of history," I said, almost instinctually.

"Exactly. And that was the subject of my next journal article, and that article helped me get the job at William & Mary." She looked over the cabin. The delight on her face let me know that restoring the cabin was enough of a reward of its own.

*

On the hike down, she filled me in on what happened to Corbin Gray. "He finished school and went back home to North Carolina, where he worked for a few years. But the pull of this place was too much. So he moved to Sherman Valley, bought a small place, and went back to living off the land."

"Is he still alive?"

"Yeah. He's in his eighties now. But I had a really hard time tracking him down. He'd kept to himself all those years, and for the longest time, I thought he was dead."

Like Clavin, I thought, and I didn't want to ask any more questions for fear of discovering more coincidences.

We reached the bottom of Jackson Hill, bantered a little more, then said our goodnights. Neither of us talked about seeing each other again, but our parting was so natural that it implied we would. I hoped so.

Chapter Five

"I've got some bad news," McKenzie said.

With that one line, the opportunity to put my career back on track crumbled. I could never have imagined a scenario where I'd be fired before I'd even started, yet it sounded like I was just about to live through one.

"I had to make some changes because the University adjusted our budget," McKenzie said. "I'm dropping your two classes from the schedule."

He looked down at the schedule of classes, as if he were still perusing it, still deciding whether this was the best course of action, even though he'd already made his decision. "I'm sorry," he said, without emotion. "But we won't be needing you this year."

My mouth went dry. Though this was well within the parameters of my contract—there was a standard clause that said my classes could be canceled at any time—this never happened unless a course didn't attract enough students.

McKenzie looked up from the schedule and waited for me to respond.

"You're canceling my classes for both semesters?" I said.

"Yes."

"Can you reconsider me for next semester?"

"I'm sorry. I can't. The budget is for the entire academic year."

"Is there a non-faculty position available?" I was desperate. I had given up my job at USC and moved across the country for this.

"I'm sorry. We don't have anything, but you're welcome to try other departments."

Of course, I'm welcome to, I thought, but I kept my anger in check. I hoped he'd offer to recommend me to another department. That would be helpful, especially at this late date.

But he didn't offer. Instead he stood up, indicating the meeting was over.

I didn't follow his lead. I remained seated. So he walked around his desk to usher me out.

"Any suggestions?" I said, a bit too aggressively, then stood up to mask it.

He opened the door. "It's a rough market and you might look at other career choices."

My jaw clenched. Anger was pushing me to defend myself, but before I dug myself into a deep hole, McKenzie said, "The job market for PhDs is bad and getting worse. That's why we've chosen to limit the number of graduates from our program."

I nodded and stepped out of his office.

"Unfortunately, even though we're all historians, we couldn't have predicted that," he said, then shut the door.

*

I might as well have been wearing blinders when I walked back to my car. None of the sights and sounds that I passed registered.

My jaw was still clenched and my thoughts were dominated by anger at McKenzie.

I told myself to get out of that frame of mind and regroup. I was officially unemployed and needed to get a job. I may not have gotten teaching gigs, but I'd always had a job.

As I drove back to my apartment, I considered and quickly dismissed calling USC to see if they'd take me back. A well-qualified candidate had already replaced me, and I knew there were no other openings on the project. Also, it didn't help that I had committed to the length of the project, ten years, but had left after four.

My best option was to look for a non-faculty position at UVA. My second-best option was to check the other colleges within striking distance. The good part was that Virginia had many colleges. The bad part was that finding a position, faculty or non-faculty, was, as always, a long shot. Especially considering that the academic year had already started.

The third option was the private high school circuit. Teaching at a public school, other than as a substitute, was out. Public schools required certification, which I didn't have.

And the last option was any job in Charlottesville, a prospect that didn't sit well. I'd always worked for a university, even though it hadn't always been teaching. If possible, I wanted to keep that record intact. It had helped me land the UVA job, and it would help me land future adjunct jobs. That is, if McKenzie hadn't permanently damaged my record by firing me.

*

I stepped into my apartment and plopped down on the couch. I was in no mood to start a job search, but when my anger toward

McKenzie started growing again, instead of stewing in resentment, I got up, grabbed my laptop, and started my search.

After about fifteen minutes on the UVA jobs website, I realized that this didn't have to be an anonymous, long-distance job search. I could go to the Human Resources office and apply in person.

So I located the office on a campus map, printed out a few copies of my curriculum vitae, and opened my front door, ready to head out, when my cell phone rang.

It was Eddie, and he didn't waste any time. He told me he was heading up to Rockville in an hour and asked if I'd changed my mind.

The calculation of the pros and cons of going with him took a fraction of a second. What did I have to lose? A day or two of job hunting. What did I have to gain? Everything I'd devoted my life to.

"I'll go," I said.

Chapter Six

As soon as we pulled out of Charlottesville, I told Eddie about my lovely morning. Not because I was looking for pity, but because I was angry. "McKenzie fired me. He said the University 'adjusted' his budget and he had to drop my classes."

"That doesn't sound right. The budget for this year was set last year."

"So you're saying he had another reason?" *Like, maybe, it was because he saw me fraternizing with you.*

"Yeah—he's an asshole."

I thought Eddie would follow that up by launching into a bitter screed, detailing how McKenzie had mistreated him. He didn't. Instead, he got right down to business. "So tell me what else you know about Clavin."

"I pretty much told you everything." I still wasn't ready to give Eddie a sneak peak at the information I was withholding. I planned to put that information into the book I'd write if I ever uncovered Einstein's secret.

"I resurrected Clavin from the dead for you," he said. "A miracle like that deserves a reward. Tell me what else you know."

He had a good point.

"I'm not going to share whatever you tell me with anyone else," he said. "But if I know what you know, it'll help when we talk to Clavin."

That was another good point. Good enough to prod me into opening up. After all, talking to Clavin *was* a coup, and he'd provided it. "It turns out that Einstein had formal meetings with Clavin," I said. "On Saturdays, on and off."

"How did you find that out?" Eddie's curiosity was palpable.

"I was able to find some of Ruth Meyer's appointment books." Ruth Meyer had been Einstein's long-time assistant, for over twenty-five years, and she'd been meticulous about keeping his schedule. She was the one who had called the ambulance, instead of letting Einstein die at home as he'd asked.

"What were the meetings about?" Eddie said.

"I have no idea. She usually penciled that information in, so Einstein could prep, but with Clavin's meetings, there was nothing."

"Do you have a theory about it?"

"Not really, but I did notice a pattern. Meyer didn't book any other appointments after Clavin's. And I don't mean for the rest of the day. I mean for the one or two days that followed. Of course, that doesn't necessarily mean anything. Maybe Einstein took those Sundays and Mondays off. But it was odd that he only took them off after meeting with Clavin."

Eddie glanced at me. "Maybe he was working with Clavin on a really complex proof and they worked on it for days. Was Clavin a mathematical genius?"

"I looked for hints of that, but couldn't find any. I guess it's possible he was some kind of savant, like in *Good Will Hunting*."

"Maybe we'll find out when we get to Rockville."

Now that I had forked over some information, it was my turn to do a little interrogating. "You said you'd tell me why there was an obit for Clavin in 1970 even though he didn't die in that car accident."

"I'm not sure I can explain that yet."

"You mean you don't know why."

"I mean that I'm not sure you're going to like the reason."

"What difference does it make whether I like it or not?"

"I don't want to sour you on this mission before you talk to Clavin."

"Guess what? Not telling me is souring me."

"I'll tell you after you talk to him. Believe me, it's better that way."

I could've whined like a baby *But you promised to tell me*, but I didn't want to argue with him. So I just stared out the window at the passing countryside. I guess you could've called it sulking. I didn't. I thought of it as showing restraint so the car trip didn't degenerate into my demanding the explanations he was clearly withholding.

We didn't talk much until we were almost there. Then we laid out a plan for questioning Clavin and, even though I'd been sulking, Eddie wanted me to take the lead. We'd introduce ourselves as social workers so we could ask Clavin about his life. Then hopefully those questions would lead to small talk and we could ask him if he'd actually read Einstein's final words on those precious sheets of paper and did he know what happened to them? If a nurse came in while we were there, we'd tell him or her that we were Clavin's nephews, out of earshot of Clavin, then make a quick exit.

*

We arrived at the hospital in Rockville in the early afternoon, well within visiting hours. We found Clavin's room on the third floor and walked right in.

He was sleeping, and that gave me time to take in his appearance. His face was gaunt and pallid. His neck, thin and feeble. Wispy white hair covered his flaking scalp. I was so disturbed by his appearance that I had to willfully force myself to ignore my natural instinct to just leave the poor man alone.

"Mr. Clavin," I said.

He didn't stir, so I leaned in. "Mr. Clavin."

His eyes blinked open a couple of times, then closed.

I tried again. "Mr. Clavin."

His eyes blinked open again, three or four times, and this time they stayed open. They had a distant, unfocused look, as if the man behind those eyes didn't know where he was.

"Mr. Clavin, we're here to check up on you," I said. "To see how you're doing. Can you understand me?"

"What?" His eyes were trying to focus on me.

"Can you understand me?"

"S-Speak up."

"Do you have problems hearing?"

He nodded.

"We're the social workers from the hospital," Eddie said, in a voice much louder than mine. Hopefully not so loud as to attract the attention of a passing nurse.

"Oh," Clavin said, but it was hard to know if he'd understood.

"We're the social workers," I repeated.

"Y-Yeah," he said, weakly.

"We wanted to ask you a few questions and find out how you're doing?" I said.

"O-Okay."

"Do you know why you're here?"

His eyes focused on me. "I-I'm sick. I-I don't g-get sick a lot."

Eddie whispered to me, "We made contact. Get into it before we lose the connection."

"Mr. Clavin, we wanted to clear up some questions about your past," I said. "There's a lot of paperwork to fill out."

Clavin's eyes wandered away from me.

I forged on. "You lived in Princeton, New Jersey before you moved to Maryland. Is that right?"

"No," he said.

That threw me off. "So you don't remember living there? I know it was a long time ago."

Clavin's eyes ticked over to his IV bags. He had three going.

I waited for him to respond. He didn't. "Do you remember living in Princeton, New Jersey, Mr. Clavin?" I said.

"I went there." His gaunt face tightened into a fragile smile.

"That's good. We'd like to ask you more about it."

"W-Where?"

Uh-oh, I thought, but forged ahead anyway. "Princeton, New Jersey. Do you remember living there?"

"I-I went there."

I glanced at Eddie. He'd resurrected Clavin, but the old guy was in bad shape. Maybe he had Alzheimer's or dementia.

"Keep going," Eddie said under his breath.

"Do you remember your job there? In Princeton?" I said.

Then, in a moment of sudden lucidity, Clavin barked out, "Who are you?"

"A social worker from the hospital."

"Oh." He stared at me and his eyes sharpened. "You're here because of Albert."

I was stunned and glanced at Eddie. "Here we go," I whispered—

Just then, a nurse walked into the room.

"Hello, gentlemen," she said. "I'm glad to see Mr. Clavin has some visitors!"

Damn!

Eddie quickly stepped up to the nurse, shook her hand, and in a low voice, said, "We're Henry's nephews."

I forced a smile her way, then looked back to Clavin, hoping to keep him focused on Albert until we could get the nurse to leave.

She moved past Eddie, over to the IVs, and checked them. "Your uncle is doing a little better than when he came in," she said. "But he's got a long way to go." She leaned down and spoke directly into Clavin's left ear. "Mr. Clavin—I'll come back in thirty minutes, so you can enjoy your nephews." Then she turned to us. "Can I have a minute with you two?"

We followed her out to the hallway where she pulled up to confer with us. "We'd like a family member to talk to his admitting doctor," she said. "Your uncle has septicemia. It probably started as a urinary tract infection, but it's spread fast."

Her words registered, but I was focused on her nametag, *Andrea.* Eerily close to Nurse Ander, the nurse who'd been on duty the night of Einstein's death. *Another coincidence.*

"At his age, infections can get out of hand pretty quickly," she continued. "And it looks like that's what happened. We've got him on an antibiotic, but it's hard to find the right one when it's gone this far, even with the cultures we're taking."

"Could he die from this?" Eddie asked.

"Easily. If we can't reverse the infection, he's going to go into septic shock. That's why we need to have a family member involved. His assisted living facility didn't have any next of kin listed." She lowered her voice to emphasize the gravity of the situation. "I'd like you to check in at the nurses' station and set up an appointment with his attending physician."

Eddie didn't respond, putting me on the spot.

"Sure," I said, still staggered by her name.

She nodded appreciatively.

"Before we check in with the nurses' station, we'd like to visit with him a little longer," Eddie said. "While he's still awake."

She looked Eddie over, and I wondered if he'd made her suspicious. "Okay," she said, then headed down the hall.

*

We walked back into Clavin's room, and he was staring right at us. "It's… t-time," he said.

I hurried over to him, "Time for what, Mr. Clavin?"

"For you to g-get it."

It? He couldn't possibly mean the secret. He didn't even know why we were here. Maybe dementia was doing the talking. "Mr. Clavin," I said. "Tell me about Albert. What do you remember about Albert?"

He closed his eyes, as if severing our connection, and I took that as a call to action. I leaned into his left ear and asked him point-blank, "Did Einstein have a secret?"

Clavin's eyes instantly opened, and I held my breath. *This is it.* I waited for him to speak, thinking he was delving into his memories, gathering his thoughts.

But after a minute or so, he closed his eyes again.

"Mr. Clavin?" I said.

He didn't answer, and his breathing became shallower.

"Mr. Clavin?"

Again, no answer.

Had my window of opportunity passed? Gone forever? I had to make contact with him, again, and get him to click back into his memory of Albert. "Did Einstein have a secret, Mr. Clavin?" I said.

Clavin opened his eyes and looked straight into mine. "It's g-good to see you again."

"It's good to see you, too." I feared I was talking to dementia, but I pressed on. What else could I do? "Mr. Clavin, do you know if Einstein had a secret?"

"He t-told me to—take it."

Oh my God. I glanced at Eddie. His eyes were as wide as saucers. We'd struck gold. My pulse quickened.

"Are you talking about the letter he wrote?" I said. "In the hospital?"

Clavin stared at me. His eyes looked distant once more, but this time he seemed to be willing forth an ancient memory, rather than wondering where he was.

"You mean Einstein asked you to take the secret?" I said, hoping to keep him on message.

"To give it to Mr. Va—" He stopped, and licked his dry lips, and I was just about to yell out *Who?! To give it to who?!* when he said, "… to Mr. Van Doran."

I was flabbergasted. A real clue. A *new* fact. *Verification.* I was rendered speechless and, if there was such a thing, my entire body was rendered dumbstruck. It took Eddie to follow up with the next logical question. "Did you read it?" he said.

Clavin turned his head toward Eddie and, though I would've never guessed the old man had the energy for it, anger flashed across his face. Then his breathing became more labored.

"You d-don't understand," he said, then turned back to me. His anger was gone. He concentrated on me with all his strength. "You—You're—" He strained to catch his breath.

I waited, hoping he'd find his voice again and finish his thought. But instead, his taut face grimaced in pain, and he fought to suck in another breath. As I watched, the guilt of treating Henry Clavin as a clue, instead of a frail man clinging to life, suddenly hit me full force. I could see from the awful contortion of Clavin's face that he was terrified. He was sure that he wouldn't catch another breath. Ever.

He was going to die. If not now, very soon.

He finally managed to take in a raspy breath, filling his lungs, and after he let it out, his breathing stabilized.

Nurse Andrea stepped back into the room. "Looks like you have another visitor, Mr. Clavin," she said.

Behind her was a big, broad-shouldered man with thick, dark hair. He was wearing a sports jacket and pressed khaki slacks. The man sized us up before turning his attention to Clavin. The man stepped up to Clavin, and as he did, I realized that he seemed vaguely familiar. Not someone that I'd met, but someone I'd seen in passing somewhere.

Nurse Andrea stepped up to Eddie and me. "Mr. Clavin's doctor is doing his rounds now, so this might be a good time for you to talk to him. And it works out great since Mr. Clavin has another visitor."

She headed out.

The last thing I wanted to do was leave Clavin's side. But we had to keep up the charade of acting like relatives, so Eddie and I both reluctantly headed out to the nurses' station. Hopefully Clavin's visitor would be gone when we came back.

*

At the station, while we waited for the doctor, Eddie brought up the visitor. "What if he's here for the same reason we are?"

"That's impossible. No one else believes my insane theory." And that was the absolute truth. No one else gave any legitimacy to the theory that Einstein had written a deathbed confession.

"It's not so insane anymore, right? Clavin pretty much confirmed it."

"But it's still a big leap to think someone else connected Clavin to Einstein's secret."

"Why? I did."

I was about to say, *but you're insane, thus proving my point,* which would've been one of those jokes with a little truth mixed in, when the doctor arrived. Without questioning whether we were Clavin's nephews or not, he immediately filled us in on Clavin's medical history, which he'd gotten from the medical records at the *Inn on the Boulevard.* It was clear that those records were spotty.

Medical records were hard to come by. As a researcher, this was one of my pet peeves. History was littered with valuable medical records, but rarely were they transferred or copied, so the bulk of them ended up discarded in history's rubbish pile.

The doctor then gave us a summary of Clavin's current condition. It was the same diagnosis that Nurse Andrea had given us. Clavin wasn't faring well, and the doctor was worried enough to ask us to go and fill out a medical directive form, instructions that told the hospital how far doctors should go to save a patient's life. This was more than I'd bargained for, but Eddie just nodded. He wanted to get back to Clavin.

"Doctor Bremer." It was Nurse Andrea, and she was heading toward us at a fast clip. "Clavin's gone into septic shock."

"Excuse me, gentlemen." Doctor Bremer hurried toward Clavin's room.

"You can wait downstairs in the waiting area," Nurse Andrea told us.

"This isn't good, is it?" I said.

She shook her head. "I'm sorry. We'll do everything we can." She headed back to Clavin's room.

I should've been praying for Clavin's health as I watched her retreat down the hallway. Instead I was asking myself, *where had Clavin's other visitor gone?* There was no sign of him in the hallway.

Chapter Seven

Eddie and I went downstairs, but opted to wait in the hospital's inner courtyard, where there was no one around to overhear us, rather than the waiting area.

"We need to find out if Clavin read the confession," Eddie said. "And if he didn't, or can't remember what it said, we go after this Van Doran lead."

I was feeling even worse about ignoring Clavin, the man. Treating him as if he were an inanimate clue was cruel. But I didn't say anything to Eddie, and continued to play the role of a detective investigating the dead annals of history. "If Clavin doesn't know what Einstein wrote, don't count on going after Van Doran."

"You know who he is?"

"*Was*, unless you're going to resurrect him, too. Of course, it's possible he's still alive. But he'd be in the neighborhood of a hundred and ten, so don't count on him being too talkative."

"So in the fifties he was closer to Einstein's age than Clavin's."

"Yep. He was an electrical engineer, a professor at Columbia. But I really don't know much else about him because I never connected him to the secret. As far as I could tell, Einstein barely knew him. They were both part of a group that met at the Princeton Club in Manhattan to talk about scientific breakthroughs. To tell you the truth, I couldn't believe that Clavin brought him up."

"An electrical engineer, huh?" Eddie was trying to add that piece to the puzzle, as was I.

"Maybe Einstein had discovered something about electromagnetism," I said. "But that doesn't explain why he picked *this* electrical engineer. He had the pick of the litter. He'd worked with some of the top people in that field."

"I have a more practical question. Why didn't Van Doran show the confession to anyone?"

"Maybe he never got it."

"Or maybe, he kept it to himself and pawned Einstein's discovery off as his."

Eddie went to his car, returned with his MacBook Air, and fired it up. He tore through the Internet searching for information about Van Doran. He unearthed both public and private records. It was amazing to watch. Eddie's hacking skills were at the level of a professional's, and that, combined with his formidable investigative skills, made for a fast and thorough ride through Van Doran's life.

I saw something peculiar, but wasn't sure if Eddie had picked up on it. It had nothing to do with electromagnetism or with Van Doran's personal or professional life. But it did have to do with Einstein's death. I didn't mention it, and Eddie waited about fifteen minutes into his search before mentioning it.

"He disappeared three days after Einstein died." The excitement in Eddie's voice said the rest. *Conspiracy.*

"That's probably a coincidence," I said, and immediately regretted using the word "coincidence." I was beginning to believe that word meant something very different. It meant "connection." Still, I persisted with my denial. "It's a stretch to think that has anything to do with the confession. *Plus* we don't know if Van Doran ever got that confession. There's no record of it. All we have is Clavin's word."

"We have to go back up there and confirm he got it." Eddie said, then looked over my shoulder. "We've got company."

I turned around. Nurse Andrea was heading out to the courtyard. "If she wants us to do something more for Clavin," I said, "say 'yes' like you mean it." Chastising Eddie was my feeble way of treating Clavin like a human being and not a clue.

Andrea stepped up to us and didn't say a word for a few seconds. A sure sign that she was here to deliver bad news.

"I'm sorry," she said in a measured tone. "Your uncle is gone. You were very lucky to have had a few words with him before he passed."

My first thought shouldn't have been a thought at all. It should've been a feeling. A feeling of sorrow. But it wasn't. My first thought was a question. *Who was the man visiting Clavin?* He must've been in the room when Clavin died.

"Will you two be taking care of the arrangements?" Andrea asked.

"Yes. We'll take care of everything." Eddie said this solemnly, as if he meant it, which I appreciated. But then he added, "Do you know who my uncle's other visitor was?"

"He didn't introduce himself."

"And you didn't pick it up when you were in the room?" Eddie's solemnness was gone. He was in interrogation mode, and he must've realized it because he then tempered his tone. "I mean, it'd be great if we could contact some of his other relatives. It'd mean a lot to us."

"I didn't overhear a name." Andrea didn't seem annoyed. Not yet.

"The truth is," Eddie said, "we didn't know much about our uncle because he was estranged from our side of the family. Maybe this can bring us all back together."

Andrea glanced toward the interior of the hospital, and at first I thought she was ready to get away from us, but then she lowered her voice. "His name was Greg Van Doran."

What?! Impossible. This coincidence was the most unnerving one yet until the rational explanation spelled itself out. The visitor must be related to Greg Van Doran, a descendant of his, a Van Doran who'd taken on the same first name. That made sense.

"Did our uncle recognize him?" Eddie said. "Or did he have to introduce himself?"

I had no idea what the point of Eddie's question was, and it looked like Andrea felt the same way. She looked at her watch and shifted uncomfortably. She was probably thinking that she'd said too much already. "I have to get back to my floor," she said. "I'm sorry about your uncle and I hope your family comes together. Family is everything."

Except when you don't have one, like me, I thought.

Andrea reached out and squeezed my arm, comforting me for losing Clavin. I accepted her gesture as if it were meant to acknowledge the loss of my own parents.

She headed back into the building.

"Gregory Van Doran, huh?" Eddie said.

"He must be a relative of the original one."

"That's one explanation." Eddie raised his eyebrows, which formed a curious and amused expression, one I hadn't seen before.

"And what's the other explanation? An impostor, like us?"

"It doesn't matter right now. What matters is that he's after the same thing we are."

If that was true, that would mean that Clavin's visitor knew as much about this little corner of history as I did. Maybe even more. That just wasn't possible. Unless he really was a relative of Van Doran's, *and* Van Doran was truly connected to Einstein's secret.

Eddie was already back on his MacBook Air, in search mode. "I'm checking out Van Doran's relatives."

While he ripped through hundreds of web pages, Andrea's words came back to me. *Family is everything.* Clavin had no family, no living relatives that I knew of, so no one was going to be "making arrangements." When my mom had died, Aunt Jeannie had "made the arrangements," and tried to do so much more. Her number one priority had been to shelter me from the blow of losing my mom.

She left her own two kids in the care of her husband so she could live with me while I finished out the school year. Then she stayed through the summer until I left for college. Aunt Jeannie stuck to my every move to make sure I didn't fall apart.

I was angry at life. My mom had died of breast cancer after guaranteeing me that she'd fight through it. I'd believed her, and I needed her to fight through it. But her decline was fast. Within six months of her diagnosis, she was gone, and I was left with the trifecta of anger, numbness, and loneliness. She had tried to prepare me. She'd told me over and over again that she loved me, and that her love would be there even after she died.

It wasn't.

Everything was hollow and empty and dead. I walked through the halls of my high school and the rooms of my house with no awareness of where I was. I hardly noticed Aunt Jeannie. She didn't try to overcompensate for the tragedy by acting overly cheery like some people did, and somewhere in the back of my numb state, I appreciated that.

Some nights, before I turned off the lights to go to sleep, she'd knock on my door, come into my room, and ask me how I was doing. I'd always said the same thing.

Okay.

She didn't follow up with more questions or with any other kinds of talk. She would stand there for few seconds, both of us quiet, and then she'd close the door and head to her bedroom. Those moments of silence were the only respite from my loneliness.

I owed her.

*

"Van Doran doesn't have any living relatives," Eddie said.

"Are you sure?"

"Positive."

"So our visitor was *pretending* to be related to Van Doran." Which meant he *did* know as much about this little corner of history as I did, and, if I was being honest with myself, probably more. After all, he'd connected the confession to Mr. Gregory Van Doran, and I hadn't.

Eddie looked me in the eye as if he had something to tell me but was reluctant to say it. After a very long three seconds or so, he said, "Let's check out Van Doran's disappearance." But I knew this wasn't what he'd really wanted to tell me. He was withholding information.

Three minutes later, Eddie was reading from his computer screen, summing up a *New York Times* article about Van Doran's disappearance, dated April 23, 1955. "Mrs. Eva Van Doran, his wife, reported him missing on April twenty-second—three days after Einstein died. She told the police that she was expecting him to return from a trip the night before. The police checked the local hospitals and came up empty. It also says that the police didn't find any evidence that he was the victim of a crime."

"What about the trip? Where did he go?"

"It doesn't say."

Eddie found a second article, dated May fifteenth, and this one was much more detailed. It seemed that the disappearance of a Columbia professor had garnered some interest. Eddie and I both started reading the article. Apparently, Mrs. Van Doran had pressed the police to do more. She'd said that her husband wouldn't just run off. He was responsible and met all his obligations. But the police said they had no leads.

Then Eddie and I must've hit the same paragraph at the same time, because I looked at him just before he said, "A connection." According to a Columbia faculty member, Van Doran had been spending a lot of time in Maryland, working on a project.

"Maryland. Clavin," I said.

"But what does that mean?"

Eddie scrolled further down the page and I saw something that made my heart skip a beat: a photo of the missing Gregory Van Doran accompanied the article.

He looked exactly like the man who'd just visited Clavin.

I leaned back, waiting for Eddie's reaction. But he stayed hunched over the computer screen. *No reaction?*

"Look at Van Doran—that visitor *has* to be related him," I said. "He must've had relatives."

"Maybe I was wrong," Eddie said. But he said it without conviction, and didn't even glance at me. What was going on with him?

He continued his search and found a couple more articles from a few weeks later. They just repeated the same information while hyping up the unsolved mystery angle of a Columbia professor's strange disappearance.

Well, at least now I knew why the visitor had looked familiar. He resembled Van Doran, and I must have seen Van Doran's photo somewhere in my research, back before I dismissed him as being irrelevant. Like thousands of people I'd gone through, he was only tangentially connected to Einstein, and he wasn't connected to the secret at all.

That thought led me to the idea of applying one of my preferred tactics, the tactic I used whenever I couldn't find any new facts. Revise history by reinterpreting the facts I *did* have.

"Can I search for something?" I said.

"Sure." Eddie handed me his laptop.

"I want to go back to Van Doran's connection to Einstein." And that meant going back to the photo where I'd first seen Van Doran. A photo I'd found many years ago. I easily tracked it down. It was a photo of a group of men taken at the Princeton Club in 1954.

Einstein was easy to pick out, and so was Van Doran. But another man caught my attention. In an otherwise straightforward photo of men in dark suits, this man stood out because his tie flashed a spark of color.

"Look at this guy," I said, and pointed to a man with a round face and sad, intelligent eyes. "Check out his tie." His tie had an orange bird on it, a species of bird I recognized. "That's an Oriole, as in the Baltimore Orioles, the baseball team—"

"As in the state bird of Maryland, right?" Eddie said.

I nodded. "Maryland, again."

I then started searching for more information about this man, listed in the photo as Harold Weldon. There wasn't much about him online. His obituary provided the most information. He'd been a very wealthy man, who'd done quite well for himself in the stock market. A kind of mini Warren Buffet, he then went on to run a couple of investment funds. He'd lived on an estate in Cumberland, Maryland, and died there in 1975.

"Van Doran was working on something in Maryland, and that's where Weldon's estate was," I said.

"And Clavin was a Maryland man," Eddie said. "I think we're headed to Cumberland." Going to Cumberland seemed like a wild goose chase, and my doubt must have been written on my face, because Eddie added, "Listen, Maryland is the connective tissue right now. I mean, you made the Oriole connection yourself."

"And what about Clavin's visitor? What about following up on him?"

"We're doing that, too."

"What does that mean?"

"I'll explain in the car."

"Last time you told me you'd explain in the car, you didn't."

"This time I will. I think you're ready."

Chapter Eight

We left the hospital without making any arrangements for Clavin. I didn't bring it up with Eddie and he didn't bring it up with me. As we headed up to Cumberland, which was less than a two-hour drive from Rockville, I tried not to think about Henry Clavin.

"Mr. Harold Weldon, the man with the Oriole tie," Eddie said. "Ever hear of him before today?"

"Nope."

"He wasn't a friend of Einstein's?"

"Not that I know of. But it's possible. I only followed up on people who I thought might be connected to the secret."

"Do you remember Weldon in that photo? I mean the first time you saw that photo."

I'd been thinking about that myself. "It was a long time ago."

"You don't think you would've remembered that splash of orange on his tie?"

"What's your point?"

"You were sure that Clavin died in that car accident, right?"

"Yeah."

"And then I showed you he didn't."

"And?"

"Do you ever think that you're right about something? I mean positively sure that you're right. But when you check back on that something, it's changed?"

"You mean that I made a mistake? So what?"

"No—I mean that something has *actually changed*. Of course, you can't be sure. And you can never be sure. Because once something changes, you can't find out how it was before."

"You're not making any sense." *Was he a nut, after all?*

"Look up Clavin's death. His car accident."

I pulled out my iPhone, but he motioned toward his laptop in the back seat. "It's got 4G."

I reached back, scooped up the computer, and after two minutes of checking, I could already tell that anything referring to Clavin's death had disappeared. The obituary, the newspaper account of the car accident, and the funeral announcement.

My face felt flushed and my mind suddenly ached. It was literally hurting with confusion. "I don't get it…"

"It blazes tiny trails at first," Eddie said. "Then, as a different history gains strength, facts change."

"What the hell are you talking about?" It was time to end this wild goose chase and head back to Charlottesville to start looking for a job. Alex's warning had been legit, after all. Stay away from Eddie. I was angry with myself for not heeding that advice.

"I'm talking about Van Doran," Eddie said. "You were stunned when you saw his photo in the paper. He looked exactly like the visitor we saw at the hospital."

"So what? Van Doran has relatives. Not a big surprise."

"He doesn't have any living relatives."

"You said yourself that you were probably wrong."

"I lied." Eddie looked over at me. "You saw yourself that it was more than just a resemblance."

I let out a nervous chuckle. "So you're saying it's the same man?"

"Yep."

Well, I knew that he'd been reluctant to tell me something. But I never would've guessed it'd be something as absurd as this. "And how do you explain that?"

"Time travel."

I took a deep breath. He was interpreting the facts in a more twisted way than I'd ever dare to do. "You know that's insane."

"You're going to help me prove it's not."

"Is that why you wanted my help in the first place?"

"Yep."

"You think Einstein's secret is about time travel."

"More so than ever, after seeing Van Doran."

"So he's a time traveler?"

"Yeah."

"And how do Clavin and Einstein and Weldon fit in?"

"I don't know yet, but my bet is that Einstein's confession ties them all together."

I looked down at the computer and brought up the Van Doran photo from the newspaper article. Then I pictured the man I'd just seen in the hospital. Without Eddie's influence, before he'd even said a word about time travel, I'd thought that these two men looked exactly alike. And what about the fact that Clavin's death in that car accident had vanished from the historical record? What explained that? And then I thought about the coincidences that had come my way since moving to Charlottesville.

It all added up to something peculiar, but how could it add up to *time travel?* It couldn't.

Eddie didn't press his point, and I was sure that he was counting on my getting acclimated to the new worldview he'd just presented. And for right now, I was a captive audience. Stuck in his car in the middle of a wild goose chase.

I started checking other facts about Einstein's secret to see if anything else had changed. As far as I could tell nothing else had.

Eddie glanced over at me. "You're looking for other trails."

"Depends on what you mean by 'trails.'"

"I mean that a 'different' history, a new one, grows slowly at first. Then exponentially. But it starts with these little trails blazing into the current history."

"And by trails, you're talking about little changes in history."

"Yeah. Kind of. I mean they're fluid. At least, I think they're fluid."

"You mean they're not permanent."

"I can't say for sure. But that's what I mean."

"So why doesn't everyone notice these changes?"

"Because they're not looking for them. And by the time a new trail takes root, they—and we—think that's the way it's always been."

"Sounds like a tough theory to prove." *Not to mention crazier than a Philip K. Dick novel.*

"Not really. Do you know what reconstructed memories are?"

"No, but I have a feeling I'm going to find out."

He laughed. "Our minds don't record things accurately. There are dozens of tests proving that we just make up a good chunk of what we 'remember.' That's why eyewitness accounts don't count for much in a court of law. And we also doubt our own memories. We actually *realize* that we don't remember things too well."

"And that's what this alternative history is counting on?"

"Yeah, but it's not an 'alternative' history. It's more like history is changing."

"Because of time travel."

"You're catching on."

"Eddie—come on. Why are you the only one who sees this?"

"I'm not the only one." He looked at me. "Take a look at that Princeton Club photo again."

I found the photo, glanced at it, and my heart started thumping wildly. Van Doran was gone from the photo. That couldn't be.

I calmed myself, took a deep breath, and leaned in close to the computer screen, but that didn't change a damn thing.

"How did you know?" I said, in a tiny voice.

"I didn't. It was just a guess. I figured he was going to cover his tracks."

"This isn't a tiny trail," I said.

"It is to the rest of the world."

He was right.

Chapter Nine

I didn't talk for the rest of the trip, and Eddie didn't try to sell me on anything more. It wasn't until we were about ten minutes outside of Cumberland that he spoke up. "Got an address for the estate?"

I looked it up, told him, and he plugged it into his GPS.

"Listen, I know Weldon's been dead for thirty years," he said, "but this is one of those trails, and we've got to follow it to get anywhere."

"Clavin was one of those trails," I said.

"That's right."

Well, I can't say that I really believed that Clavin was one of *those* trails, the kind of trails that Eddie was talking about, the kind that blaze a new history into our existing history, but I did believe one thing. I had followed the Clavin trail and it had proved its worth. It had confirmed that Einstein's secret was real. And that was Eddie's point.

"So somewhere in Weldon's estate is the next clue to finding Einstein's confession," I said.

"That's my bet."

Neither of us said anything about time travel or about Van Doran being a time traveler. And that was fine by me.

Eddie skirted the town of Cumberland to get to the two-lane road that led to the estate, which was a few miles farther west. Cumberland had been a big manufacturing center, but it had long since fallen on hard times and was now part of one of the poorest counties in the country.

We passed a few houses, almost all of them run-down clapboard homes in disrepair. Then we hit a long stretch of forest, broken up only by an abandoned drive-in movie theater. And judging by how large the parking area and screen were, it must've been quite the attraction in its day.

A mile later, a tall iron fence appeared on the other side of the road. It penned in the woods that made up part of the Weldon estate. The fence eventually gave way to a large gate.

Eddie pulled up to the gate, and behind it, at the end of a garishly long driveway, I saw a sprawling Georgian mansion. It needed a paint job and cosmetic work, but it clearly had once boasted great wealth. Next to it was a much smaller structure, either a large garage or stable, or combination thereof.

Eddie scanned the side of the gate for a call box. "So we keep this simple. We tell whoever's home that we're doing a story on Cumberland's most famous residents, and that we'd like to talk to one of Weldon's relatives."

"Good plan, except we have to get through the gate." There wasn't a call box.

"We need to track down the phone number." He pulled out his laptop and started his search. It didn't take long for him to pass judgment. "The Weldons of Cumberland like their privacy."

"No number?"

"Not even an unlisted number." He closed the laptop. "We're going to have to go in there unannounced."

"They're not going to be too receptive to us if we surprise them."

"We can't wait."

"Why not?"

"Facts are changing. If we don't follow this trail now, we'll lose it."

Again, I couldn't help but think that this was the plot of a Philip K. Dick novel. Except this time it felt like I was living that plot, because I had the weirdest epiphany: I doubted that Clavin had ever died in that car accident. Didn't it make more sense that he'd died today, at the hospital? After all, I'd seen him there with my own eyes, and that was a fact.

Had I ever actually seen his obituary? Or his funeral announcement? No, I hadn't. There was no evidence that he'd died in a car accident.

I made myself stop this chain of thoughts. The new history was playing on my doubts. Reconstructing my memory. Just as Eddie had said it would. But I wouldn't let it. As long as I had this strange awareness of facts competing for reality, for the historical record, I thought I could control my memories.

Eddie got out of the car and tried to fit through the spaces between the gate's iron railings. He couldn't. Then he looked to the top of the iron gate, but I could see that climbing over it would be impossible.

He got back in the car. "We're going to have to walk the length of the gate and find a way in."

*

We continued down the road until the fence ended. Then we pulled off onto the dirt shoulder. Eddie opened the car hood, as if we'd had car problems, but that wasn't our problem. Our problem was that the iron fence ran all the way into the woods, not just along the road.

So we started walking its length, into the woods, hoping it would end soon enough. It didn't. A few trees on our side had limbs growing over onto the other side, and those limbs were increasingly looking like our way in, though not an easy one.

The iron fence finally gave way to a wooden split-rail fence, three feet high, that ran along the back of the Weston property. We walked along it until we were behind the mansion, then climbed over it. As we approached the back of the mansion, the forest thinned out, and it ended at the edge of what must've once been an expansive lawn. It was now overgrown with wild grass and weeds.

At the other end of the lawn was a patio that ran along the back of the house. Eddie started toward it, fearless, but when he saw me hanging back, he stopped. "I can check it out alone. It's up to you."

"You planning on breaking and entering? Or going around to the front and knocking?"

"Not sure yet."

As I weighed whether I wanted to add breaking and entering to my resume, Eddie ran across the weedy lawn as fast as he could, minimizing the chance of being spotted from the house. At the back of the house, he positioned himself against the wall, between two of the five sets of French doors that bordered the patio.

He looked back at me, waiting for my next move.

I scanned the marble patio. It was weather-beaten, cracked, and barren of furniture, matching the desolate look of house.

No one lives here, I thought, and used that rationalization to sprint across the lawn.

I joined Eddie, and he leaned over and peered into the French doors. "Hard to tell, but it might be abandoned," he said. "Let's check some of the other windows."

Each window told the same story. The rooms were furnished with grandiose pieces, in keeping with the Georgian design of the house, but all the opulence looked dull and defeated, as if no one lived there. Either the house had been abandoned, or Harold Weldon's descendants were terrible housekeepers.

We checked the windows and doors to see if any of them had been left unlocked. None had. At that point, I thought Eddie—the treasure hunter, the commercial archeologist—would come up with a clever way of breaking in. But he went with the old standby.

He took a loose brick from a pathway that ran behind the smaller structure, which turned out to be a combination garage and storage building, wrapped the brick in his T-shirt, and with one quick hit, smashed through a window on the east side of the house.

We waited to see if someone emerged from the bowels of the house in response to the shattering glass. No one did. Eddie unlocked the window, slid it open, and we climbed into Harold Weldon's mansion.

We were in a sitting room furnished with antique couches, high-backed chairs, and a grand piano. The paintings on the walls depicted lush rolling hills, like the hills you'd find around Cumberland.

I felt uneasy about this whole endeavor and wanted to quickly find a clue that would make sense of this morphing quagmire, then get out. A document, a photo, some kind of record—anything that would put us one step closer to Einstein's confession.

"I'll check upstairs," Eddie said, as he headed out of the sitting room. "You take the downstairs."

I scanned the room, and at first, nothing caught my eye. Then I saw that the piano bench had a hinge on it, so I walked over to it and opened it.

It was empty.

Then I checked inside the piano itself and saw nothing but the strings and hammers.

I turned to the door and my breath caught in my throat—

Van Doran was standing in the doorway, holding a gun to Eddie's head. "What did Clavin tell you?" he said.

"Nothing," I said, barely able to get that out because my heart was thumping so wildly, once again, that my entire body was shaking.

Van Doran jammed the barrel of the gun into Eddie's temple. "You want me to kill your friend?"

"Clavin didn't say anything." I sounded weak.

"You're lying."

"I'm not lying."

Van Doran started to squeeze the trigger, and I spoke loudly and confidently. "I'm not lying. Clavin was incoherent. I couldn't get him to tell us anything."

Van Doran stared at me with a punishing glare. It turned into a condescending smirk before he said, "I didn't think you were talented enough to put it together." He nodded at Eddie. "No doubt this man played a role."

How the hell does he know anything about me?

He shoved Eddie forward. "Now, I've got a problem. Two more loose ends. You obviously know way too much." He aimed the gun at my chest, ready to fire—

"Clavin did give us a lead," I blurted out.

He hesitated.

I pulled out my iPhone. "It's recorded right here."

That gave Van Doran just enough pause for me to tap the iPhone a couple of times. "And now five of my friends have a copy of that lead. In case something happens to us."

Van Doran kept the gun trained on me. "You're stupid. You're not saving yourself. You're putting more people in jeopardy."

"And giving you more loose ends," Eddie said.

Van Doran looked at Eddie. "I can take care of—"

I hurled my iPhone at Van Doran and he instinctively jerked out of the way, which threw off his aim as he fired the gun. I lunged at him, and we both hit the floor and wrestled for control of the gun. Eddie kicked the gun out of Van Doran's hand, sending it sailing across the room.

I was about to chase after it, when Eddie yelled, "Let's go!" He took off into the hallway and I followed.

"You're a brave man," he said.

"Fear of dying does that to you."

We raced down the hallway, past a deserted study, where I caught a glimpse of a desk and a couple of dusty easy chairs, then down another hallway, when I heard a gunshot—a warm breeze blew by my cheek—the bullet—and I sprinted as fast as I could into the kitchen.

Eddie slammed the door shut behind us, but there was no lock. Another shot rang out, hitting the door with a thick thud. Eddie ran over to the kitchen table. "Help me!"

We pushed the table over, slamming it up against the door just in time. Van Doran pushed on the door from the other side, but we leaned into the table, barricading ourselves in.

"We're going over there," Eddie barked out, craning his head toward the back of the kitchen.

Across the worn, yellowed linoleum floor, between grimy cupboards, I saw an open door leading into darkness. "If it's the basement, we'll be trapped."

Van Doran slammed against the door.

"You bailed us out the first time," Eddie said. "Let me return the favor. Trust me on this. Go on."

I let go of the table and raced toward the darkness. Eddie let go, and Van Doran's next shove edged the table forward and left the door ajar. He fired a shot through the opening.

Eddie sprinted my way as the table shrieked forward. Van Doran was barreling in—

I bolted down the stairs and saw pure black ahead of me. But I didn't stop running. There was no time to think about what was up ahead. *So this is what I do with my career opportunity at UVA* was my only thought as I sprinted farther into the dark. I glanced back to see if Eddie was behind me, when another shot rang out—

I saw Eddie stumble at the bottom of the stairs, and just then, before I could react, everything around me went white and undulating, as if I were running through an ocean of pure, white, glowing energy.

It felt hot and prickly, and went on into infinity in every direction.

Had I been shot and not Eddie?

There was nothing around me but this atmosphere of thick white sea. I kept running, even more panicked than before.

Am I having a seizure?

I was sweating hard, and the white ocean was getting even hotter. I couldn't breathe—the oxygen around me was suddenly depleted.

I doubled over, trying to suck in air, choking, surrounded by what felt like raging white flames. I was sure this pure white sea would burn me alive. But before it did, I passed out.

Chapter Ten

"Jacob."

Someone was shaking my shoulder.

"Jacob, let's go."

I opened my eyes, and the memory of what had just happened flooded into my consciousness. I was already plenty confused and mighty groggy, and the fact that an anomaly was staring me right in the face didn't help my condition—

Alex was looking down at me. *What the hell was* he *doing here?*

"We have to get out. Now," he said.

I slowly sat up and saw that I was in a small room equipped with a desk and bookshelves. Then I noticed the stone wall to my left. Was I in a carrel in the Caves? *Impossible. This had to be Weldon's basement.* But his basement had seemed much bigger than this. And where was the staircase?

"We've got to go," Alex said.

I wobbled as I tried to stand up, so Alex helped me to my feet. "What happened?" I asked.

Alex moved to the door and opened it. "Come on." He stepped out into a tunnel. *One of those tunnels.* The stone tunnels under the Lawn at UVA. The Caves.

But I'm at Harold Weldon's estate.

I made my way out of the carrel and into the tunnel, and Alex locked up. He then started down the tunnel at a good clip. I tried to keep up, dragging a little. If there was any doubt left as to where I was, it dissipated when I saw the battery-powered lights and dead pipes.

Was I hallucinating? Maybe I was lying on the floor in Weldon's basement, dying from a gunshot wound. That made sense. The alternative didn't: that I'd passed out in Weldon's basement and awakened in the Caves.

"Alex, what the hell is going on?"

"Let's just get out of here, first."

"What are you running from?"

"It's a 'who'—not a 'what.'"

Van Doran, I thought. But why would Alex be running from Van Doran? He knew nothing about him. I was the one who was running from Van Doran.

As we moved through the tunnels, I looked for signs that this was a dream. Unfortunately, my steps struck hard against the ground, and there was nothing dreamlike about that.

The same with Alex. There was nothing dreamlike about him. I hadn't seen him since last winter, when he'd picked me up from Dulles for my interview with McKenzie, but nothing had changed about him. He was true to his character: focused. And right now that focus was on getting out of here.

We had talked many times since our college days, and had even visited each other at grad school a couple of times. But even though we were good friends, I'd been totally surprised by his offer to recommend me at UVA.

And grateful.

During the three days I'd stayed with him in Charlottesville, I'd found him to be just as focused as he'd been in college and grad school. Getting the appointment at UVA hadn't changed him. He was still up at five a.m., writing and researching.

He'd always been a great student, but even so, when I read the acclaimed biography he'd written, it was hard to believe that my college buddy had created such a detailed and entertaining work. He had the ability to make historical figures come to life. It was a great payoff for his hours of hard work.

During my visit, he'd been working on his newest biography and I'd hoped to get a peek at it. But he wouldn't say a word about it. He thought it'd be a jinx if he talked about it before he finished the first draft. The only thing I found out was that it was the reason for his sabbatical next year, and, therefore, the reason I was getting this interview at UVA.

His reticence was probably due more to his upbringing than to superstition. One night during our sophomore year in college, over Christmas break, when neither of us had gone home for the holidays, he'd opened up about his family.

I'd already known that his parents were upper-class WASPs from Connecticut who hadn't been involved in his life, nor in the lives of their other kids. What I hadn't known, until that night, was that as soon as Alex had left for Deerfield, a prestigious boarding school in Massachusetts, his parents had as much as abandoned him.

He said that they saw it as a way to teach him that he could live on his own, but for a fourteen-year-old to learn that his parents didn't expect him home for Thanksgiving or Christmas anymore... That was a bad blow. A blow that hurt. He'd been the only kid at Deerfield to stay at the school over Christmas.

And when he went home that first summer, he found that his parents had already left for a brownstone they owned in Paris. He was left alone, with two housekeepers. His older brothers weren't there. They had long ago learned not to come home.

He returned to Deerfield without seeing his parents at all that summer. They didn't return from Paris until after school had started. From that point on, he made every decision about his life and his studies on his own. His parents gave him a monthly allowance and paid his tuition, but otherwise, they weren't involved in his life at all.

His opening up to me that night had bonded us for the rest of our college years and beyond. Not just because we were both kids without parents, but because we both had stories we wanted to keep buried.

*

Alex scaled the slots in the wall, pushed the trap door open, then hoisted himself up into Grace Hall. He motioned for me to hurry up. I kept my curiosity in check, which wasn't easy, and climbed the wall.

We headed to the first floor, exited the building, and just as I was ready to pepper him with questions, a bone-chilling wind hit me full throttle. That was a shock. And more shocking was the sight of the barren trees against a sky thick with gray clouds.

The August heat was long gone. It was winter.

How long had I been unconscious?

Students were walking briskly along the brick paths, bundled up in coats, and, for the first time, I registered that Alex was wearing a thick sweater. New questions were piling up before I'd even started with my original ones.

"Alex, what's going—?"

"It's December, six months ago for you, and you're back in Charlottesville. When you were visiting me from L.A."

"Time travel."

I said it, but I wasn't buying it. Not yet anyway. I reached into my pocket for my iPhone, to check the date, then remembered that I'd used it as a weapon.

Alex checked behind us, still on the lookout for whoever was after him, or us. We made it to the Corner and started down University Avenue, passing the small shops. Alex was hyper-aware of his surroundings, glancing in all directions.

I veered into a coffee shop and grabbed a copy of the campus newspaper from a stack by the door—and the date confirmed Alex's story. I spotted a copy of the *New York Times* on a table. Its owner was gabbing on a cell phone, so I lunged forward and snatched the paper up.

"Hey, I'm still reading that!"

I checked the date, and the *New York Times*, the paper of record, confirmed Alex's story. My eyes quickly ticked over the news items to see if I recognized the stories as belonging to this past December.

I did.

"Hey, asshole, I haven't finished with that."

I dropped the paper back onto the table, and my mind wanted to process this, it really did, but my body was interfering. I suddenly felt queasy and unbearably exhausted. My body wanted to go to sleep and wake up healthy and ready to look for that new job.

I forced myself to go back outside.

"Satisfied?" Alex said.

"Satisfied probably isn't the right word."

Alex started down the sidewalk, expecting me to keep up. I barely did.

We passed Greenley's, where Eddie had first reeled me into this nightmare, and that brought back a more recent memory. It hadn't been me who'd been shot in the basement. At least, I didn't remember it that way. It had been Eddie who had stumbled after the gunshot rang out.

"What happened to Eddie? He was with me at Weldon's."

"This is his fault."

"What?"

"Well, isn't it? That's why you're here."

I couldn't argue with that.

Alex turned the corner and hurried to his car. "We can't go back to my place. It's too risky."

"Too risky because someone is after you or too risky because there's another one of me already there, waiting for his job interview?"

"Both."

Finding out there were two of me running around didn't do much to convince me that this was really happening. Two of me seemed like a time-travel trope. And that was a problem. Because the part of me that was beginning to accept time travel desperately wanted to discover that time travel wasn't at all like it'd been depicted in science fiction. For some reason, that would've made it easier to accept.

What I didn't know then was that I'd get my wish. Time travel *wasn't* like science fiction had depicted it. But there'd be no joy in discovering that. There'd be just the opposite. I'd be desperate to have some time-travel tropes as my guide.

*

I climbed into Alex's car, and he immediately pulled out and headed away from campus. He still hadn't explained much—as in nothing—but I was starting to accept this new reality. So much so that I realized Alex had been hiding something from me, and he must've been hiding it for a while.

"You knew that Einstein's secret had to do with time travel." How else could he have known about the time machine? "That's why you recommended me for the job."

"Yeah."

I felt betrayed, and if my stomach hadn't already roiled with queasiness, my anger would've had room to grow. "You knew getting Einstein's secret was basically my life's work and you didn't say anything?"

"It's a long story."

"Then why don't you get started?"

"I will, but first you need to understand one thing. I don't know what the secret is."

"You know it's about time travel."

"I don't."

"Give me a break." Was he trying to cover up that he'd stabbed me in the back?

"Listen, I'm not denying the time travel. I'm just saying I don't know what the confession is about."

"I'm not following you at all."

"I'll walk you through the short version."

"Okay…"

"You connected Clavin to Einstein."

I nodded.

"And you ended up at Harold Weldon's estate?"

"Yeah." Wow. He was hiding way more than I thought.

"But that doesn't mean that Einstein's confession has anything to do with time travel. All you know is that time travel has to do with Weldon."

"It all starts with Einstein."

He glanced at me with a knowing smile. "Do you have proof?"

"Of course." I had that photo, which connected the two. Of course, that same photo used to connect Van Doran to Einstein, too, and I knew damn well what had happened to *that* connection.

"Is your proof online?"

I nodded, and he handed me his iPhone. I searched for the photo, feeling doomed, and when it came up, my queasiness grew tenfold, overwhelming my incipient anger. I magnified the image, just to make sure. There was no doubt about it.

Weldon was no longer part of the photo.

The only familiar member of the group was Einstein. This photo was no longer evidence of any connection between Weldon and Einstein.

That fact was now gone.

Einstein is the key. I had to hold on to that. But I could already feel the doubts creeping in, reconstructing my memory. Of all people, I latched on to Eddie for help. He'd thought that Einstein's secret had to do with time travel. And he'd been right. Hadn't he?

"How did you find the time machine if it wasn't through Einstein?" I blurted out.

"The Caves. I was assigned that carrel. At first, I didn't notice anything. Then in the middle of one long night—I'd been researching for forty-eight hours straight—I thought I saw someone appear and then quickly disappear. Into the wall. I was in kind of study daze, so at first I thought maybe I'd fallen asleep. But then it happened again a week later." He took a breath. "Here's the thing: I was there a lot. So I'm sure that whoever had been using it was surprised that the damn place was never empty anymore."

I believed the part about him studying down there all the time. But the rest of his story... "So it was all random? You get this carrel and it just happens to turn out to be a time-travel machine? You were never looking for it?"

"First of all, it's not a time-travel 'machine.' It's some kind of portal. And, yes, it was random. No one in The Cabal has ever said anything like, 'Hey, we've assigned you a carrel that doubles as a time-travel portal.' And I sure as hell wasn't going to bring it up."

Alex was now on the outskirts of Charlottesville.

"Where are we going?" I asked.

"You're going to stay in a motel, and I'm going to see if anything else goes wrong. If we're in the clear, you're going back."

"What do you mean 'go wrong'?"

Alex turned into the parking lot of the Valley View Motel, a rustic motel on Route 29. "Shit—*that's* what I mean." He nodded over to the only other car in the parking lot and instantly started to swing our car around, accelerating into the turn, setting the tires squealing.

As I lurched to the side, I caught a glimpse of the driver behind the wheel of the other car, a broad-shouldered man with thick dark hair.

Van Doran.

Alex rocketed out of the parking lot. "I don't know who he is. The first time I saw him, I thought he was following me, but I wasn't sure. The second time I was sure."

Alex didn't know it was Van Doran. But I didn't understand how that could be if he knew about Weldon. *Because this isn't connected to Einstein.* That was his point. Wasn't it? The facts in my head were jumbled and I couldn't sort them out.

But I didn't pipe up. I didn't tell Alex that I knew the man behind the wheel of that car. I was withholding information from him as he'd done from me. Except that my information was beginning to seem faulty. Not facts, but conjecture.

Alex checked the rearview mirror and I looked back.

Van Doran was pulling out of the parking lot.

"Why are you running from him?" I asked.

"Because the second time I saw him, he threatened to kill me if I didn't go back."

With the words "go back," I suddenly understood why Alex's biography on Eisenhower had been so detailed and entertaining. It teemed with life because he'd gone back in time and experienced that life himself.

"You went back to the fifties. That's where you saw him."

Alex sped up. I checked the side-view mirror again. Van Doran's car was gaining on us.

"That's right," he said. "But the second time, I barely made it back here."

So his story was starting to make sense, but the big picture was getting foggier. "I don't understand how he could be here, Alex. He was the guy who just hunted me down through Weldon's house."

"You already know how."

And I did. "There are two of him. At least. Just like there are two of me, right now."

"One on the run and one at my place," Alex said, "relaxing before his interview with McKenzie."

He raced through a stop sign and ran up behind some cars. Instead of slowing down, he swerved into the lane for oncoming traffic. The lane was currently clear, but talk about out of character. Alex wasn't in control anymore. He was running for his life.

I checked the side-view mirror. Van Doran was right behind us.

Alex veered back into the right lane, but Van Doran didn't follow. He stayed in the lane for oncoming traffic and sped up beside us.

"What's he do—?" I managed to blurt out before Van Doran's car rammed into us and sent us fishtailing and skidding.

Alex fought to keep control of the car.

It swung around a hundred and eighty degrees before it came to a sudden stop, facing the wrong direction. The car bearing down on us slammed on its brakes, trying to avoid a head-on collision, and the cars behind it followed suit—

Howling tires, followed by the harsh thud of one car hitting another, filled the air. And then the scene went silent.

The accident was somewhere behind the lead car, which had thankfully missed hitting us.

I glanced around, checking for Van Doran's car, but didn't see it.

Alex was desperately trying to start our car. He fired it up on the third try, lurched forward, then skirted around the motionless cars, now scattered askew, passed the two cars that had collided, and headed back the way we came.

When the mess passed into the rearview mirror, I finally spoke up. "How can he pull crap like that without changing history?"

Alex was looking at the rearview mirror. "Looks like you might get a chance to ask him."

I glanced back. Van Doran was bearing down on us again.

"We can't shake him by car," Alex said. "We're going to have to lose him on foot."

He turned back onto Route 29. There was more traffic here, but Alex had four lanes to work with. "Darden Towe Park is up ahead. It's acres and acres and we can lose him there."

Alex weaved around the traffic. Van Doran kept up, then Alex pulled a sharp right into the park. He raced through the parking area, past tennis courts and playing fields, until he landed on a service road.

The road led us to the less-developed section of the park. First picnic areas shaded by woods, then hiking trails through the forest.

We passed a sign that read *Access to the Rivanna River*, and Alex said, "We're going to make a run for it. As soon I stop, get out, and head into the woods."

I looked back. Van Doran's car was about forty yards behind us.

Alex rapidly decelerated. "Keep the sun to your back and you'll be heading east. It gets pretty wild in there, so he'll give up pretty quickly." He suddenly pulled over and brought the car to an abrupt stop.

I jumped out, started toward the woods, and glanced back to see something I would never forget.

Van Doran didn't slow down. He was speeding up, bearing down on Alex, who was about to round the front of the car. The thud I heard was sickening—Alex's body flew forward, and Van Doran kept going.

As I ran for Alex, whose body was now thirty feet down the road, Van Doran's car disappeared around the curve up ahead. He'd done what he'd come here to do.

I knelt down next to Alex's body. His torso was twisted ninety degrees from his pelvis. Blood was pooling around his head, and his eyes were open, glassy, and blank. I was trembling uncontrollably and had to turn away.

How can he be dead? He's alive. I'm visiting him right now, this weekend.

Something had definitely gone wrong.

And I had to fix it.

Chapter Eleven

Still trembling, I headed toward Alex's car. I didn't realize I didn't have the keys until I was behind the wheel. So I got back out and forced myself to approach Alex's body by purposely squinting to blur my vision. I didn't want to take in his wrecked frame again.

I reached into his pants pocket, and as I pulled out his keys, I also felt his iPhone in there. I took it, too, instinctually knowing I'd need it. I ran back to the car and slid in behind the wheel. By the time I'd turned the car around and was heading out of the park, my mind was awash in hopelessness. Nothing good could happen anymore. I fought to push back an unrelenting sadness. The sadness that had hung over my life after my mom had died.

But the picture of Alex's body, lifeless and twisted, abandoned by the side of a country road, was seared into my mind.

I'd abandoned him. Like *I'd* been abandoned.

Once I was on Route 29, I forced that image of Alex out of my mind and told myself that he was still alive. After all, wasn't he? In the real history, the correct history, he must be.

He had warned me not to follow up with Eddie. That's how this nightmare had started. Or had it started with Einstein? With my own obsession?

Trying to answer those questions now was pointless. The truth was that I had no idea what was going on.

Should I call the police and report Alex's death? Only if this was real; but it wasn't. It was some strange history that was writing itself over the real history. The real history that I had to get back to.

I have to fix this.

I'd head to the Caves and go back to nine months from now, and everything would by hunky-dory. That's how time travel worked.

Didn't it? Or was it possible that I'd go back to the future and find that Alex *had* been murdered?

I couldn't be sure, one way or the other, but going back seemed the right thing to do. I could fix things from there.

So how was I going to get into Alex's carrel? I looked down at the ignition and realized that I had all his keys. But the relief didn't last but a second.

How would I get into the Caves? I didn't have the combination to the trap door.

And that led back to Eddie. At this point in time, I hadn't yet met him. That was still nine months away. Nevertheless, he was the best option.

Then a new obstacle reared its ugly head. Alex hadn't told me how the time-travel portal worked. How could I be sure I'd end up nine months from now, where I belonged?

*

About three miles from Darden Towe Park, a fire truck and an ambulance, sirens blaring and lights flashing, raced past me. There was no doubt where they were headed.

Two miles later, three shrieking police cruisers roared by, and it was then that I realized just how stupid it had been to take Alex's car. Too late now. I'd dump it in town, then track Eddie down.

I kept a lookout for Van Doran's car, but didn't see it. Maybe he'd called it a day after killing his number one threat. After I reached the Corner and parked, I pulled out Alex's phone and searched for Eddie's address. Luckily, his place was only a twenty-minute walk from campus, so I no longer needed to risk driving Alex's car.

As I headed over to Eddie's, I wondered about the repercussions of using Alex's phone after his death. What would the police make of that? I convinced myself that it didn't matter because this version of history was going to disappear.

*

Eddie's house was a ranch-style, with the rundown appearance of a rental, familiar to anyone who's ever lived in a college town. I knocked on the door, and a blond woman in her early thirties greeted me.

I asked for Eddie and she went to get him.

On the walk over, I'd had a little time to figure out what I was going to say. I'd decided to hang my hat on the fact that Eddie already knew something about my bizarro world. After all, he'd been the one who'd approached me about Einstein, and it'd turned out that he'd known a lot more than he'd let on.

But now, standing here on the threshold, I realized this wasn't a given. Maybe he'd learned everything in the months leading up to my arrival in Charlottesville. If that were the case, convincing him to believe in my bizarro world was going to be a tough sell.

Eddie appeared, and I introduced myself as a friend of Alex's from grad school. Then I said I had something personal to talk to him about.

He stepped out of the house and closed the door behind him.

This was the moment of truth. I would just tell him what happened, in chronological order. But that's not what came out of my mouth.

"Alex is dead," I said.

Eddie grinned, as if he thought I was joking.

But I didn't crack a smile.

Seconds went by as I held his stare. He lost his grin. "I'd know if Alex was dead."

"Go ahead and check it out." I'd seen the police racing to the scene of the crime. If the local news was doing its job, there'd already be something posted online.

Eddie didn't move.

"If I'm lying, I'll leave."

"Okay, I'll take a look."

He turned to go, and it dawned on me that Alex's actual name might not be posted yet. "It'll be a report about a fatal hit and run. In Darden Towe Park."

Eddie left me on the stoop. Knowing him, I was betting that he'd find out the victim's name by hacking into the private communications of the police, fire, and local news.

He returned two minutes later, looking shaken and pale. "How did you know? The name hasn't been released."

"He was murdered—and it's because of what's in his carrel."

"What's in his carrel?"

It was too soon to launch into the entire time-travel saga. "I can't tell you yet. I have to show you something first."

"So show me."

"We have to go to Alex's house."

"I'm not going anywhere."

It was time to take advantage of the one time-travel trope that Alex had confirmed was true. "Eddie, if you go to Alex's house, you'll find another version of me in there."

"Wow, really?" That contained a perfect blend of disdain and sarcasm. "Why don't you get out of here?"

I remembered that the other Eddie had been curious about why Alex wanted to keep his carrel after graduating, so I used that next. "Doesn't Alex seem way too protective of that carrel?"

"Yeah, and I thought that's what we were talking about. Not some bullshit about your clone."

"This *is* leading to the carrel."

"How?"

"If I explained it to you now, you'd have me locked up as a loon."

"You *are* a loon."

It was time for my Hail Mary pass. Time to bet on a long shot. "Listen, you know something is up. And you don't really need me to confirm it, do you?"

He cocked his head, and I knew I'd hit my mark.

"What do you mean, I know something is up?"

"You were checking out an event, or a place, or a document. I can't tell you exactly what it was and I can't tell you when. Maybe you were looking at it today or yesterday or last week, but here's the thing: you noticed that some detail had changed. And you were *sure* it changed. You remembered it one way, but it wasn't that way anymore. The only problem is, you can't prove it. There's no longer any evidence of the way you remembered it."

His eyes had gone wide and there was just a glint of fear in them.

"And now you're wondering if you were wrong," I continued. "You're thinking that your memory might be faulty."

"Okay," he said. "Let's head over to Alex's place."

*

When we turned onto Alex's block, we saw two unmarked police sedans parked in front of Alex's house. Here was another element I hadn't thought through. Eddie drove right past the sedans. Only a fool would voluntarily get involved in an active police investigation.

Eddie turned onto the next block and pulled over.

"You're going to have to go in there without me," I said. "The officers aren't going to be too keen on seeing two of me." I'd used my best weapon on him—the trails that time travel blazes into history. My fate was now in his hands.

"I'll check it out," he said, and got out of the car.

As I waited for his verdict, I couldn't help but wonder if the reason Eddie went on to develop an interest in Einstein and time travel was because of me. I was the one who'd told him about it. Tonight.

But that didn't make any sense. Nine months from now, when he approached me in front of Grace Hall, I didn't know anything about time travel. So how could I have introduced it to him?

He introduced it to *me*.

Was it another version of me? Or had history changed? Or—

Before my head exploded with questions, I pulled out Alex's phone to look up theories of time travel. I did hesitate for a second as I pictured a homicide detective discovering that, just after Alex's death, someone had used his cell phone to research time travel.

The detective would never in a million years guess that this was a valid clue. The clue that could break the entire case wide open.

At first, I found only one time-travel theory that took into account the strange world I'd entered. It was the multiple timeline theory. In essence, it said that traveling into the past created a new and totally different timeline, starting at the point where you arrived back in time.

The other timeline still existed, the one from whence you came. It still existed and went on about its business. But after digging deeper, I discovered that this model of time travel didn't account for a new version of history blazing trails into the old version. In this model, each timeline was separate and unique.

I was about to move on to another model when the driver's side door whipped open and Eddie slid in. "The cops were questioning you and Alex's roommate about the accident. The *other* you." He keyed the ignition, pulled away from the curb, then turned to me. "What the hell's going on?"

"Time travel."

"Time travel, huh? What about twins?"

"You think that was my twin back there?"

He didn't answer. His eyes stuck to the road.

"Just tell me that you have enough doubts about the twin theory to check out Alex's carrel."

"How does the carrel fit into this?"

"It's a time-travel portal."

"You're making the twin theory sound pretty good. What about Alex's death? How does that fit into your sci-fi extravaganza?"

"It's a result of the extravaganza. And I have to fix it."

"How?"

"I don't know. But I know Alex is alive in the future, and maybe that means I *do* fix it. Or did fix it. Or will fix it."

"How far in the future?"

"Nine months from now. And I'm going back." I didn't mention that I had no idea how to program the portal.

Eddie didn't ask another question for a few long silent moments. I wondered if his curiosity had been piqued enough to get me into the Caves, or if he really believed that he'd just seen my twin.

Finally, he spoke up. "I'll take you to the Caves, but I can't get you into Alex's carrel."

I pulled out Alex's keys, satisfied that I was on my way back to the future. "We don't have to break in."

"How'd you get those?"

"Alex gave them to me."

"He just handed the keys to time travel right over to you?"

"He had to." I didn't want to explain that I'd taken them off of his dead body. "He was dying."

He glanced at me. "You were there?"

"Yeah. We were being chased."

"Let me guess: by another time traveler."

It was getting to the point where my piecemeal answers were sounding more and more absurd, so when Eddie parked the car and demanded to know everything, I filled him in. As I did, I realized that we'd reversed roles. He'd been the one who'd come to me with the Clavin lead and his insane time-travel theory, and he'd been the one who'd led me into this quagmire. Now, I was returning the favor.

But when I got to the part about Harold Weldon, Eddie interrupted my tale. "You don't mean *the* Harold Weldon?"

"I don't know—What do you mean 'the' Harold Weldon?"

"In the thirties, he was an undergrad here. It was his idea to turn the tunnels into study carrels. He founded the Cabal."

When we'd discovered that the man in the Princeton Club photo sporting the Oriole tie was Harold Weldon, Eddie must've known *exactly* who he was. That was why he'd been so eager to drive up to Cumberland. And that meant Eddie had lied to me. Just as Alex had.

But I didn't get angry at this Eddie. He wasn't the one who'd lied to me—at least not yet. Instead, I went on and told him about the rest of my adventure, and concluded, for myself, that Weldon must've found the portal in the thirties. That explained how he'd made a fortune in the stock market. Time travel pretty much guaranteed a good return on investment.

As soon as I wrapped up my crazy tale, Eddie spoke up. "If that portal really exists, I'm going with you."

Not only was that a huge leap from his earlier skepticism, it was also a terrible idea. Two of us traveling through time would most definitely lead to twice as many disasters. But I didn't say so. I didn't want to discourage him from opening up that trap door. First things first.

*

We entered Grace Hall and descended into the basement.

As Eddie moved closer to opening that trap door, I weighed whether to tell Eddie the part of my tale that I'd left out. The part that might dissuade him from going through the portal. I hadn't told him that he might've been shot in Weldon's basement. I'd just said that I'd gone through the portal first.

We took the stairs into the sub-basement. Eddie kneeled over the trap door, punched numbers into the keypad, then lifted the door open.

Once we were down in the tunnels and on the move, I thought of another reason to tell him what had happened at the end in Cumberland.

Shouldn't he know that he might've been shot before traveling anywhere? Who knew what kind of effect that would have on this trip?

We passed other carrels, all with their doors closed, except for one, where a woman was hunched over her computer, lost in her private world. Then we came to the darker stretches of the tunnels. We were approaching Alex's carrel, and it was time to tell Eddie the biggest flaw in my plan to fix things.

"I don't know where it's going to take us," I said.

"It always goes to Weldon's estate, right?"

"No—that's not what I mean. I'm sure that part is right. That's why Weldon built his mansion there. What I mean is that I don't know what *time* it'll take us to."

"You probably punch in a date."

"I didn't see anything like that in the carrel, and Alex called it a portal, not a machine. And on the Cumberland side, I just ran into it, without activating anything."

"Then that's what we'll do. Run back into that wall."

I let out a laugh.

"What's so funny?"

"I can't think of a better metaphor for this whole damn thing than running into a solid wall."

We made it to Alex's carrel, and I unlocked the door. Inside, the room was just as I'd left it. As Eddie moved up to the far wall and pressed his hands against it, I locked the door behind us.

"It's solid," he said.

"You still want to run into it?"

He didn't answer. He was busy examining each stone, pushing on them one by one.

I went over and did the same. Again, I weighed whether to tell him that he might've been shot. In my head, I tried to remember exactly what I'd seen before going through the portal. And that reminded me of something critical. *Remembering* was important. The very act of *remembering*.

I had to get that across to Eddie.

"Time travel, or time, or whatever you want to call it, counts on us forgetting," I said. "It counts on our doubts and reconstructed memories. When I told you that I knew you'd seen something change, but you couldn't be sure if you remembered it correctly in the first place—that's exactly how it works. You have to remember the way things are. The way they should be."

"Okay…" he said. He looked at me like I was a babbling lunatic.

And that's what time travel and the new history were counting on—

I heard the sound of a lock clicking, whipped around to the door, realized that someone was unlocking it, and immediately lunged forward and re-locked it.

"Time to run into a solid wall," I announced.

Eddie positioned himself as far from the wall as possible.

"Einstein's secret," I said. "Remember that. That's how this all started, and that's the only way to fix this."

Eddie hesitated for a fraction of a second, hopefully to focus on that, then ran toward the wall. His body moved right through it.

As I took off, full speed ahead, telling myself *Einstein's secret is the key*, I heard the lock click open behind me, right before I was engulfed in a sea of white.

It glowed and undulated like it had the first time.

I kept running, and I felt that overwhelming heat, but I wasn't as panicked this time. Sweat formed on my brow as the temperature rose. I was having a hard time breathing, but went with it, taking smaller breaths rather than trying to gulp the thin air.

I kept running, and suddenly the ocean was gone.

Eddie was right in front of me, collapsed on the floor. I should've told him about the heat and lack of oxygen. Too late now. He was sweating and sucking in air, but he hadn't lost consciousness.

"Just relax. You'll be okay," I said. I glanced at our surroundings, a dark room with a hint of light from somewhere above. We had definitely left the Caves. But had we moved through time?

Chapter Twelve

My eyes adjusted to the dark and I saw light above us, seeping in from under a door. There was no doubt that the light was from Weldon's kitchen, and that I was in his basement.

My next move was to scan the basement floor, a cracked concrete slab, hoping to spot the original Eddie, and also hoping he was alive. But the only Eddie here was the new one, now standing up and checking out his new surroundings.

"Did we make it?" he said.

"Yes." I looked back to the wall, fearing the person who'd entered the carrel behind us was on his way. "And we need to get out."

I hurried to the stairs, and Eddie followed. He pulled out his cell phone. "Are we back to where you started? Nine months in the future?"

"I have no idea." We hurried up the stairs.

"No reception," he said.

I opened the door, just a crack, to see if anyone was in the kitchen…

The change was obvious. The linoleum floor was bright white, sparkling with freshness, and the cupboards gleamed, shining with pride.

Even though I wasn't sure the coast was clear, I decided to take my chances rather than wait and see if whoever it was who'd entered Alex's carrel had chased us through the portal.

I stepped out into the kitchen with Eddie in tow. "Follow me."

As I headed into the back hallway, a plan, simple though it was, took shape. We'd get out through the French doors, hike through the woods, get off the property, and regroup. I ignored that I was a long way from figuring out how to fix things. My main thought amounted to this:

Don't forget what I know. Einstein is the key.

The back hallway also appeared revived. The paint was fresh and the throw rugs were vibrant with color. We turned down the next hallway, the one leading to the sitting room, and as I moved past the study, an elegant, gold sculpture of a tiger caught my attention. That slowed me down enough to notice that it was sitting on a desk littered with books and papers.

Then my eyes fell on a blackboard near the desk. Equations were scrawled all over it, and it didn't take a genius to recognize that they were physics equations. Maybe I'd been in denial when it came to the rest of the house, but seeing this made it abundantly clear that the Weldon mansion was no longer abandoned.

I was tempted to abort our getaway from the house and head right into the study. Those physics equations, for me, rightly or wrongly, signified only one person.

Einstein.

But I moved on, and Eddie was right behind me.

As we were about to pass the sitting room, I heard voices emanating from inside. I stopped short. We couldn't pass the room without being seen. We'd have to find another way out.

I motioned to Eddie and we headed back down the hallway, then down another hallway, until we hit the dining room, where the floor, cabinets, and dining room table—which must have been long enough to seat thirty people—were covered in paint tarps. Paint cans and paint trays were stacked up in one corner of the room.

We hurried through the dining room into the living room, which was decked out with opulent furniture. Every grain of wood in this room, whether it belonged to the floor, the trim, or the furniture, was polished to a high sheen. Every inch of the upholstery and every cushion was immaculate.

We'd traveled to a time when the estate was in full use. The only question was: *When?* The possibility that we'd traveled into the future seemed remote. It just didn't seem possible that Weldon or his descendants had come back to Cumberland and revitalized the estate.

We were somewhere in the past.

I opened the front door, stepped outside, and was greeted by three bloated, boat-like cars, polished to a shine, all curves and fins. Iconic symbols of an era, they left no doubt as to what decade we'd landed in.

"A Buick Roadmaster, a Lincoln Premier and a Chrysler Imperial," Eddie said, staring wide-eyed at the three cars parked in the driveway. "Welcome to the fifties."

I was stunned, though I shouldn't have been. This was my second journey into the great unknown. But the fifties? Come on, that seemed outlandish. Well, at least I wasn't panicking. Not yet, anyway.

Eddie had a tiny smile on his face, as if he were amused, as if he were experiencing a Disney ride, rather than a mind-bending scientific anomaly. Maybe he didn't quite believe that this was real, or maybe he saw this as a chance to explore the fifties, his area of commercial expertise.

I looked past the cars, down the long driveway, and was disappointed to find that the iron fence still surrounded the property. I supposed it was possible that we could have opened it from this side, but still thought it'd be safer to head around back and exit the property from there.

We made it to the back of the estate, and I was greeted by another surprise. One that I should've expected. The patio's marble surface was no longer weather-beaten, but glinted nobly in the sunlight; and the expansive lawn was no longer wild and weedy, but was green and manicured and decorated with flowerbeds bursting with blue periwinkles and yellow petunias. Rows of large pink azalea bushes in full bloom bordered the sides.

I'm not sure if this scene of overwhelming life was the tipping point or not, but it suddenly hit me that I was headed in the wrong direction. I had spent more than a decade of my life hunting down Einstein's secret, and now here I was at the heart of it all, perhaps at the very spot where everything happened: in the nineteen fifties, in this strange house in Cumberland, Maryland, where I'd just seen a blackboard full of physics equations.

Running was the wrong move. "I'd like to find out what was in that study," I said.

"Thought you'd never ask." There was no hesitation in Eddie's voice.

I broke into a smile. "If we're going to fix anything, we need to find out how the portal works, and that study is the place to start."

"One of us has to draw whoever is in there out here, and one of has to go back in there and search the study." Eddie's treasure hunter side had kicked into gear.

"So who does what?"

"I'll go in if you want—I'm used to this kind of work."

"You mean breaking and entering?"

"And the most important part: searching."

He was right. But my bet was that he wanted to go back inside to peruse the bonanza of fifties memorabilia. It was probably worth a fortune.

"But I'll be able to tell if something in there has to do with Einstein's secret," I said.

"I thought we were looking for the portal instructions."

"It's connected."

He looked back at the house again, and I came at him with another argument, his own argument from the future. "Eddie, the reason you took me to see Clavin in the first place and didn't go it alone was because I was the expert when it came to this remote part of history."

"And that didn't work out too well, did it?"

It had worked out even worse than he'd thought. He'd been shot. *And I need to fix that, too.* "I've been working on this for twelve years," I said.

He looked over the mansion. And when he took in a deep breath and let it out slowly, I knew he was going to acquiesce.

"I want you to remember two things when you get in there," he said. "Be patient. Once you've taken the risk, you might as well let things play out."

"And the second thing?"

"I know the fifties, and my take—and this is one of the many things McKenzie and I disagreed on—is that this was an era of less suspicion and more neighborly trust. Even with the systemic discrimination and the Communist cold war paranoia, this really is a more innocent time. Whoever's in there, once I draw them onto the patio, they're never going to suspect that you're inside, right under their noses."

*

The first thing we did was scout out the woods on the far side of the lawn for a place to meet up afterward. Because the property was now well groomed, that place turned out to be fairly far away.

With that done, we overturned some chaise lounges on the back patio and moved others to the middle of the lawn.

Then, though both our cell phones (mine being Alex's) had no reception, we used them as old-fashioned watches and coordinated our moves. In seven minutes, I'd be in the house, at the end of the hallway, ready to go into the study, and Eddie would start rapping on the French doors, drawing whoever was inside, outside.

Then I'd go into the study.

Seven minutes later, I was standing in the dining room, on one of the paint tarps that covered the floor, ready to head down the hallway.

I heard the rapping. Eddie wasn't fooling around. It was loud and continuous, demanding a response.

Voices rose from the sitting room, and seconds later footsteps rattled down the hallway, heading toward the back of the house.

So far, so good.

When the footsteps had completely receded, I hurried down the hallway, and was just about to step into the study, when I heard someone clearing his throat. One man had stayed behind, and he was in the study.

I quickly headed back down the hallway, through the dining room and the foyer, and out of the house. This time, instead of circling around the side of the house, I circled around the garage, not wanting to end up anywhere near the patio when I got to the back.

That worked out well. I found myself on the other side of the azalea bushes. I skirted along them, moving toward the back of the property. Through the pink blooms, I caught glimpses of the patio, so I slowed a bit to see if Van Doran or Weldon were out there.

Two men were on the patio: one standing, looking over the lawn, and one righting the chaise lounge. And though I was thirty yards away, there was no doubt about who the man looking over the lawn was.

Albert Einstein.

The shock of seeing him stopped me dead in my tracks. I didn't dare breathe for fear of ruining this preposterous moment. After a minute or so of gawking, I checked out the other man, expecting to see Weldon or Van Doran.

It was Henry Clavin. *A young and healthy Henry Clavin.*

Had Einstein been discussing the physics of time travel with Clavin? Was Clavin some kind of savant after all?

Just then, a third man stepped out onto the patio. *Weldon.*

He walked up to Einstein and they exchanged a few words. Then he looked out over the lawn, into the woods, fixating on something. After a few seconds he turned to Clavin, who'd just finished righting the chairs, said something to him, and pointed to a spot in the forest.

The spot where Eddie was hiding.

Clavin headed across the patio, onto the lawn, and toward the forest. Apparently, although people may have been innocent in the past, they weren't stupid.

I stood stock-still, hoping to avoid discovery, and hoping that Eddie was fleeing. Weldon scanned the woods for another minute or so, then he and Einstein retreated back into the house.

I had no idea how long Clavin would search the forest, but I wanted to catch up with Eddie as soon as possible. Plenty could go wrong with us on the run together, but if we got separated, that would spell disaster.

Heading toward the back of the property would present the risk of running right into Clavin, so I raced east instead. The forest eventually thickened, and as I dodged tree trunks, one question ran through my mind. How was I going to fix anything when things seemed to be getting worse?

I made it to the iron fence that ran along the side of the property and headed toward the back. I kept a lookout for Clavin, in case he'd taken his scouting mission out this far, and for Eddie, and made it to where the fence ended without seeing either.

There was no wooden fence across the back of the property, so it must've been a later addition. As I was wondering if that could've affected where Eddie had retreated to, I heard a "hey" and spun around.

It was Eddie's voice, but I didn't see him.

"Up here," he said.

He was standing on the branches of the tree above me, clutching the trunk. "Treasure-hunting experience. No one ever looks up."

"Where's Clavin?"

"Was that the guy who came looking for me? The guy you said I resurrected?"

"Yeah."

Eddie started shimmying down the tree trunk. "He turned back."

I walked over to the other side of the fence. "Let's get out of here."

Eddie caught up to me and we headed toward the road. "What did you find in the study?" he said.

"I wasn't able to get in. Weldon hung back."

"But wasn't that him who came out on the patio at the end there?"

I didn't respond because I knew what he was getting at and didn't like it.

"Why didn't you wait?" he said, getting to his point. *Be patient.*

"How was I supposed to know he'd head out?"

"Because that was the plan."

"The plan didn't work."

"It looked like it worked to me."

"Okay—so you should've gone in. You would've waited. Now we're going to have to try again."

"It's going be tough to break in a second time. Our diversion put them on notice."

"We've got no choice."

Chapter Thirteen

I may have been mad at Eddie for calling me out, but he was right. If I'd waited a minute or so more, Weldon would've left the study. Next time I'd have to think more like a commercial archeologist and less like a scholar. Research was one facet of this journey, but so was action.

Proper action.

Besides, what was the point of being mad at Eddie when it was looking more and more like Alex was the one to blame for this mess? He was the one who'd used the portal in the first place. He was the one who'd recommended me for the UVA job, not because he was doing me a favor, but because he'd wanted to find out if Einstein's secret was about the portal.

The sun was setting and the forest was swathed in amber light. That soothing glow helped me focus on the next step—getting back into Weldon's estate and searching that study—rather than blame others for my own failure.

Our footsteps crunched the underbrush, and neither of us spoke. Soon I found myself thinking about the bigger picture, not just the mission at hand. The building blocks of history. The facts. The kind of facts that were rock solid, documented, and confirmed. The kind of facts that never changed. Only the interpretations of those facts changed.

But if all facts changed, then there was no history.

There had to be some facts that didn't change and never changed. And those facts kept the whole shebang together.

Einstein is the key. His secret is the key.

"Eddie, do you have any ideas about how to get back into that house and into the study?"

"We have to scout the place first."

"Like common criminals."

"Common criminals would just break in again. Scouting the place is a little more sophisticated. I say we wait until tomorrow so we can scout the place in daylight. And there's always the chance that they'll leave during the day."

Waiting until tomorrow seemed like an eternity, but right now, trudging through the forest of 1950s Maryland, I didn't have an alternative. At least, not yet.

*

We made it to the road as dusk descended. The amber light had faded and stars were starting to dot the sky. Night hadn't fallen yet, but without the light pollution that the next sixty years would bring, the stars were already way brighter than any I'd ever seen.

With more than ten hours to kill before daylight, it was time to find a place to regroup. Headlights were approaching from a distance, and I was suddenly conscious of what we were wearing. Blue jeans, T-shirts, and sneakers.

"Let's stick to the woods instead of the road. I don't think we came dressed right."

"We'll pass. Grown men didn't usually wear jeans and T-shirts, but even in the fifties some people refused to grow up."

"Sounds like a rationalization."

He laughed. "It is. If we can't get back right away, we'll need new threads."

The headlights swooped past us without slowing down. It was another one of those oversized sedans, but this time Eddie didn't call out the model.

A few more cars passed, and Eddie asked, "What's down this road?"

"In sixty years, not much. So I'm guessing not much now."

But past the treetops, about a half-mile up head, I saw a bluish light flickering above the forest.

"What do you think that is?" Eddie said.

My first thought was based on conjecture. It was an overpowering floodlight from one of the isolated houses out this way. My second thought was based on fact. It was that shuttered drive-in that I'd seen on this road.

"It's a drive-in," I said, *and it's no longer shuttered.*

Eddie upped his pace. "Sounds like a perfect place to regroup. I wonder what's playing."

A wave of cars passed us, and as we moved closer to the drive-in, I saw much more traffic from the other direction. People were pouring in from town.

It wasn't much longer before huge, orange neon letters announced that we'd arrived at the *Oriole Drive-In*. If I'd been with the original Eddie, he would've made the same connection I did, to a certain photo and a certain man's tie. More synchronicity.

The title of the night's feature was right below the neon, *This Island Earth*. "Wow," Eddie said. "You picked a great night to go to the movies."

"We're not going to the movies."

"I'm going."

"We can't risk it. We have to lay low."

"It's not going to be the end of the world if we see a movie. I'm not going to pass up the chance to see *This Island Earth* with the audience it was intended for. In case you didn't know, it was a big-budget extravaganza that made history, cinematically speaking, and you're a history professor."

It was clear that Eddie wanted to soak up the fifties.

"We can't risk changing history even more. What if we change it so much that we can't go back?"

"The changes are already happening. Remember the trails? That's how you convinced me to help you. Watching a movie isn't going to make things worse."

Eddie walked toward the drive-in.

I hesitated, then caught up with him.

We stepped up to the chain-link fence that separated the woods from the huge lot. The lot was a whirlwind of activity. Cars were maneuvering into spaces, groups of teens were hurrying to and from the concession stand, and families were setting up lawn chairs and picnics in front of their cars. An animated short was unfurling onscreen above the commotion.

"You're not planning on lifting some collectables from in there and bringing them back," I said.

"Are you a time cop now?"

"Just sayin'. Your lucrative business is based on fifties memorabilia, and you've hit the jackpot."

"How do you know about my busin—Oh. I told you in the future."

"Eddie's Emporium."

"Well, I must've been a real talkative fellow." He looked back to the screen. "Check that out."

On the massive screen, an animated polar bear was singing "Rock-a-bye Baby" to a ferocious guard dog. The cartoon was hand drawn, the traditional way, with no CGI. It was sumptuous, rich and warm.

"That's *The Legend of Rockabye Point*," Eddie said, "nominated for an Academy Award."

"Hey, you gotta pay!" someone shouted from the other side of the fence.

I looked down and saw a kid walking toward us. He had the bluest eyes I'd ever seen, eyes that seemed strangely familiar.

"You can buy walk-in tickets," he said when he reached us. "This one's worth it."

Not only did the kid's eyes look familiar—so did the kid. I moved closer to the fence and read the shiny, plastic nametag pinned to his shirt.

Richie Morgan.

My pulse quickened and my legs went wobbly.

How can this be happening? I was face to face with my dad.

Chapter Fourteen

"How much is a ticket, little man?" Eddie said.

"Twenty-five cents for walk-ups."

I forced myself to remain steady. What the hell was this about? I didn't understand time travel, but at least running into Einstein made some kind of sense. This didn't. Why was my dad here?

Eddie reached into his pocket, checking for change. "I think we can afford it. We'll come around front."

Riche started to walk away. "Enjoy the show!"

"Richie," I said.

"Yeah?" He turned back.

I had to talk to him. If running into Einstein made some kind of sense, then running into my father must've, too. Even if didn't know why.

"I want to talk to you about something," I said.

He approached us again. "What is it?"

I didn't know, yet.

Eddie looked at me, curious, as if he wanted to know, too.

"Harold Weldon," I said.

Richie moved closer. "What do you want to know about him? My dad used to work for him."

Maybe this was going to come together after all. "We're writing a story about Mr. Weldon for the Pittsburgh Gazette," I said. "He won't talk to reporters, so it's hard to get any information about him."

"You're reporters?" Richie looked us over, as if he were just noticing that our sneakers weren't quite right and our haircuts didn't quite fit in. "You don't look like reporters."

Not a good start. "We pretended to be Weldon's cousins from California," I said, hoping that would explain our odd style choices. "But he still wouldn't talk to us."

Eddie shot me another strange look, and I wanted to tell him that it was his turn to be patient, that this was my dad, and to let me play this out.

"You said your dad used to work for Weldon?" I was hoping to get Richie back on topic.

"Yeah. But not anymore."

"What'd he do?"

"He painted some of the rooms."

I remembered the tarps in the dining room. "Isn't the place still being painted?"

"Yeah, but…" Richie looked down, avoiding my eyes. He was ashamed of something. His dad—my grandfather—must've been fired.

"That's okay," I said. "I hear that Weldon isn't the easiest guy to work for."

Richie looked up at me. "It wasn't fair. That's all."

"What do you mean?"

"It wasn't his fault that he heard them all talking about a treasure."

"That's why he was fired?"

Richie nodded.

"What kind of treasure?" Eddie said.

Richie suddenly took a defensive stance, squinting his eyes and tightening his jaw. He must've thought Eddie doubted him.

"My mom didn't believe my dad, either," he said, anger in his voice. "She said it was another one of his crazy stories. But she's wrong, you know. My dad isn't crazy."

With contrition on his face, Eddie glanced at me. This time he'd screwed up.

"Your dad is right, Richie," I said. "I know that for a fact."

Richie's jaw slackened. The possibility of finding an ally had turned his anger into hope.

"Do you know what the treasure is?" he said. "'Cause I don't."

It was the portal. "No, but I know that it really exists."

Richie stared at me for a long time, as if he were deciding whether he could trust me or not.

Finally, he blurted out, "And you won't believe this part."

"Try me."

"My dad saw Albert Einstein at Mr. Weldon's house."

"I believe you. That's why we're here."

A smile took over his face. "So it's true? My dad was right?"

I nodded.

"Wow!" Richie was now giddy with excitement. "I told Mark and Danny and they didn't believe me. They're like my mom. They never believe anything my dad says."

My heart went out to him. The young boy had his own battles to fight. I knew that my grandfather, his dad, probably suffered from mental illness. I remembered my mom telling me that.

Eddie looked at me, as if to say, where are you going with this?

"Einstein's here because of the treasure," Richie said. "Right? That's what my dad says."

In this case, mental illness or not, Richie's dad was right. One hundred percent on the money.

"That's what we came to find out," I said.

"You want some help?"

Yes, I thought, but kept my mouth shut. Wasn't recruiting my father into this the most insane risk of all?

"Yes," Eddie said. "We want your help."

Richie looked at me, instead of Eddie. "Will you promise to write the truth in the paper if I help?"

The kid wanted a quid pro quo, and I imagined him waiting for our article to come out, then rushing to get copies of the paper when it did. He'd show the article to his mom and his friends, proving once and for all that his dad wasn't crazy.

But there'd be no article.

"It's a deal," Eddie said.

Just then the crowd clapped and all three of us looked up to see the credits rolling on the animated short.

"I love this job," Richie said. The screen's flickering light reflected in his blue eyes, and I recognized the joy there. It was the same joy that I'd seen in that movie theater, when he was the grown-up and I was the kid, and we'd both laughed and laughed and laughed.

I now understood the reason for my dad's love of films. He'd found solace and stability at the movies. His family had moved around a lot, but the movies must've always been there for him. He'd taken me to the movies so I could experience that same comfort and joy.

"I gotta get some things done before the movie starts," he said. "I'll meet you in fifteen minutes at the storage shed next to the concession stand."

He took off, and Eddie and I headed toward the drive-in entrance.

"You just recruited my dad."

"What?" Eddie stopped and, for the first time—including both versions of Eddie—his face went pale. "It can't be. You just think it's your dad because of some freaky residual effect of time travel."

"It's him."

"How is it possible that you didn't know your dad lived in Cumberland? It doesn't add up."

I'd been thinking about that, and it did add up. "My dad's family lived in Pennsylvania for a while, and Cumberland is less than ten miles from the Maryland/Pennsylvania border. I don't know exactly where he lives, but I'm positive that it's nearby, just across that border."

Running into my dad couldn't have been just a coincidence. It had something to do with time travel, and I thought about explaining all the other coincidences to Eddie, but realized that was unnecessary. This one was big enough to make the point. But what exactly *was* the point? I hadn't figured that out, and that worried me greatly.

"I'm not so sure involving my dad is the best plan," I said.

"Right now it's the only plan. Let's see what he has to say."

"We're sinking deeper into the swamp."

"Then let's at least enjoy tonight's feature presentation before we go completely under."

*

As we walked alongside the line of cars waiting to get in to the drive-in, I couldn't help but think about my dad, not as the kid I'd just seen, but as the adult that I had never known.

Right after he'd died, I thought he wasn't really dead. I thought he'd come back. And not as a zombie, but exactly the way he was. At four, I didn't know what a zombie was, and I didn't know what death was. I expected my dad to walk back into our house any day.

Around five or six, I started to understand that he wasn't coming back. I felt this overwhelming sense of loss. Like a piece of me was missing and that piece contained happiness. Then I realized: if I didn't think about him, that sense of loss disappeared. So I started building a fortress around myself to keep any thoughts of him away. That fortress was completed in fourth grade.

After that, I stayed inside my fortress and didn't dig into my father's story. Sure, my mom talked about him, but it made *her* sad, too, so she didn't talk about him too often. She's the one who'd told me about his home life as a kid, and though she never said it directly, it was clear that his dad, my grandfather, wasn't a well man.

She told me that his dad had fought in World War II, but hadn't been one of those GIs who'd returned home and adjusted to civilian life. He hadn't fulfilled his destiny as a member of the Greatest Generation. His story was more like the stories we hear about nowadays. He was a war vet who had a hard time jumping back into civilian life. He couldn't hold down a job, and probably suffered from undiagnosed PTSD.

But now, somehow, his troubled life was strangely connected to Einstein's secret. One of the jobs that he couldn't hold down was painting Weldon's mansion. So it wasn't enough that history now recorded that my dad worked at a drive-in in Cumberland, Maryland. History now also recorded that *his* dad had crossed paths with Einstein himself.

Synchronicity was out in full force, and that thought triggered a theory. What if synchronicity was a real "force"? What if it wasn't just strong coincidences? What if synchronicity was a powerful energy, an energy that changed facts? What if it had changed facts about my family?

Maybe that's what synchronicity was. History changing itself and making connections where none existed before.

But why would it do that?

I pictured a powerful vortex sucking me deeper into the world of Einstein's secret, and rearranging facts as it spun its own new history.

*

We approached the drive-in's entrance, where we had to walk much closer to the waiting cars. I feared we were pressing our luck. Surely someone would notice we were out of place and point an accusing finger out the window, shouting, "Get them!"

But I ended up staring at the carloads of teens and families far more than they stared at us. As Eddie had mentioned, we were protected by the innocence of this era. Outsiders weren't embraced during this decade, but neither were they feared. Everyone was far more interested in getting inside the drive-in, finding a parking space, and loading up on concessions.

We were three cars away from the ticket window when I realized that instead of running through abstract, complicated theories of history, I should've been thinking about simple reality.

"They're not going to accept our money," I said.

"Not all of it, but we lucked out on the price of admission. The face of the quarter hasn't changed much, and I've got two of them." Eddie waited for the car in front of us to pay. "But don't plan on any popcorn."

We stepped up to the ticket window. Eddie handed his two quarters over to the cashier and received two walk-up tickets in return.

Inside, we didn't see the storage shed, but easily spotted the bustling concession stand. We headed that way, passing an endless stream of happy kids carrying burgers, hot dogs, popcorn, and ice cream. They paid no attention to us. When we got closer to the concession stand, I noticed a large patch of open ground where people sat in folding chairs.

"That's the walk-up section," Eddie said. "Fifties nostalgia always leaves that part out. Not everyone drove cars to the drive-in."

"We're not staying for the movie. We talk to my dad, then leave." We were getting way too involved with the past without knowing what we were doing or how the portal worked.

"There's the storage shed," Eddie responded, rather than fight me about staying.

The storage shed was over to the side of the concession stand, at the back, away from the hustle and bustle. Just as we got there, the movie screen went dark and the din of excited voices hushed. A few seconds later, the film started.

I wanted to talk to Eddie about the conversation we were going to have with my dad, to establish some parameters so we weren't interfering with my dad's history, but Eddie was already glued to the screen.

Cal Meacham, a famous pilot and scientist, the main character in *This Island Earth*, was flying his jet across the country. Right before landing, his plane suddenly lost power. Then a mysterious force, which made the plane glow an eerie green, took over the controls and safely landed the jet.

Just as Cal was deboarding his plane, Richie showed up and jumped right into a quid pro quo. "I'll help you get into the house and you tell everyone that there's a treasure in there."

"We might not be able to find it," I said.

"Then tell everyone that Einstein was there. Put it in the paper."

"That, we can do," Eddie said.

"Then you've got a deal." Richie was gung ho to prove to the world that his dad wasn't crazy.

I shot Eddie an annoyed glance. I wasn't so keen on making any promises.

"I know how to get into the house," Richie said. "Mr. Weldon has these glass doors along the back."

"The French doors?" Eddie said.

"Don't know what you call them—they're the doors along the patio. The lock is broken on one of them. The one all the way to the right."

"The right from the inside or outside?" Eddie asked.

"Outside. So you'll tell everyone that Einstein was in Cumberland, right?"

This time Eddie hesitated before answering, but he answered all the same. "Of course."

Richie grinned, then looked at the film. He watched until the scene ended, then said, "I've got to work the concession stand now." Apparently he told time by where he was in the film.

But before he took off, I wanted a better farewell. This would now become my last memory of my dad. And instead of the joyous memory I had, looking up to him in the movie theater, this one had ended on a broken promise.

"Richie, it doesn't matter whether other people believe you or not," I blurted out.

He looked at me with a frown, as if he was confused. I had lobbed a complete non sequitur at him.

"A fact is a fact," I added. "That never changes just because someone doesn't believe it."

This time, he nodded as if he was considering my statement. And the weird thing was that I was considering it, too. Weren't facts now subject to change? Except I was referring to a fact that wasn't going to change. There'd be no newspaper article confirming that Richie's dad was telling the truth.

"But when it's in writing, everyone knows it's true," Richie concluded, as if he'd figured it out.

I didn't argue with him. He was right. *When it's in writing, everyone knows it's true.* History has to be recorded. Whether it's recorded correctly or incorrectly, it's the only way history has a chance to exist. And when an event disappears from the written record, it's no longer part of history.

He adjusted his shiny, plastic nametag, *Richie Morgan*, then started toward the concession stand. "Good luck, you guys," he said over his shoulder.

Eddie turned back to the screen. "Now that we have a way in, my vote is to go back tonight. Weldon and crew will be tucked away, sleeping."

I knew exactly where he was going with this. "Meanwhile, we stay and watch the film."

"Why not? We have to wait till the middle of the night, anyway."

I didn't argue. But it wasn't because I was convinced by Eddie's reasoning. It was because I wanted to talk to my dad one more time. It still felt like I was leaving him with a lie. Because I was.

From the shadows of the shed, Eddie and I watched the rest of film. In the end, Exeter, the alien, sacrificed himself to save Cal and Ruth, the humans. As I watched that, I had to wonder if alien mythology was as misleading as time-travel mythology. Whoever said that truth is stranger than fiction was right. Time travel was far messier than the way it was portrayed in fiction, and I guessed that this would hold true of real alien life.

As the credits rolled, I spoke up. "You'd think that time travel would be some kind of grand discovery, but it doesn't feel that way."

"We don't know enough about it yet."

"We don't know *anything* about it." But I hoped in the next few hours, after checking out that study, we'd know a lot more.

Eddie wanted to stay for the second feature, *All That Heaven Allows*, but I convinced him to head out. He conceded that so far we'd managed to fly under the radar, but if we stayed and contended with the mass exodus at the end of the night our cover might be blown.

I never did try to speak to my dad again, which I regretted as soon as I'd left the drive-in and trekked into the woods. But what I didn't know then was that this encounter with my dad had ended far better than our next encounter would.

Eddie and I hiked back to the iron fence and down along it, toward the back of the Weldon property. When we made it to the woods directly behind the mansion, we waited. There was no reason to approach the house until it was well past midnight. Our plan was to break in and spend thirty minutes searching the study.

"If we don't find anything, we head back to our time and plan out our next trip here," Eddie said.

"It's tough to head back if we don't know how to use the portal. Who knows what time period we'll end up in?"

"It worked out okay this time."

"It didn't work out okay when Alex was killed."

"But what about running into Einstein? That wasn't too shabby."

He had a point. But it wasn't enough to convince me to blindly jump in again. "Ending up in the fifties didn't put us any closer to fixing anything."

"It put us closer to Einstein's secret, right?"

Chronologically speaking, he was right, but that was it. "Things are getting worse, not better. Running into my dad doesn't seem right. Like history is changing more by the minute. I say we stay until we find Einstein's secret."

"You're saying that Einstein's secret and the instructions for using the portal are one and the same."

"I didn't come up with that idea; you did."

"Huh?"

"The other you—the one who dragged me into this—thought that the secret had something to do with time travel."

"What exactly did I say?"

"That was about it. I didn't believe you so I didn't press you."

"You should've believed me."

"I wish I had."

*

A few hours later, at two a.m., we hiked up to the edge of the manicured lawn.

The house was completely dark.

We ran up to the French doors on the far right, where I turned the knob and gently pushed on the door. It opened. Richie had done his part.

The inside of the house was as dark and silent as the outside. We made it to the study without a hitch.

But here, we had to take one big risk, one that we could've avoided. We hadn't secured a flashlight even though the drive-in had been loaded with them. Eddie blamed himself for this. He was the treasure hunter and knew the tools of the trade.

I flicked on the study light, and light spilled out under the door, into the hallway, and through the curtainless window into the yard. With our presence now literally spotlighted, Eddie and I quickly dove into the papers and folders on the desk. The small sculpture of the golden tiger watched us.

I was expecting to find mathematical equations, proofs, and theorems—and I did. They were there aplenty. But I was also expecting to find theories about how the portal worked.

There weren't any. *Not a one.*

I looked over to see how Eddie was doing. He was making his way through a stack of files, betraying no emotion.

"Anything?" I asked.

"If you mean have I found a set of operating instructions—Nope."

I found more proofs and calculations, then finally came across some speculation, written out in longhand. I read through it, then riffled through more folders, and found more speculation.

As I read more and more, I began to pick out a pattern, and it wasn't the pattern I wanted to see.

The speculation and mathematical proofs were all about the various theories of time travel. The fixed time theory, where you *can't* change time, the dynamic time theory, where you *can* change time, and the multi-universe theory, where every change created a new timeline.

There wasn't one bit of material about the portal itself and how it worked. And not only that, there were no conclusions about which theoretical time-travel model applied to the very real time-travel portal right there in the basement.

I started looking through the desk drawers.

The middle one had articles detailing Einstein's mathematical proof that confirmed the existence of the Einstein-Rosen bridge, the forerunner of what was now called a "wormhole." It predicted that "bridges" might exist between one period of time and another period of time.

This was undoubtedly why Weldon had sought out Einstein in the first place, and that was confirmed by what I found in the bottom drawer. It was packed with handwritten and typed letters. I dug through them and discovered that they were all replies from Weldon's friends and business associates: replies to letters he'd written to them.

I kept digging because I knew that Einstein had been fond of writing letters, and sure enough, I found five letters from Einstein to Weldon. These letters were the stuff that made the careers of history professors.

I picked out the one with the earliest date and read it. Even without Weldon's side of the correspondence, it was clear that he'd invited Einstein to visit the estate. Einstein politely declined the invitation.

In Einstein's second letter back to Weldon, the scientist again declined. But Weldon must've added specific information to the second invitation because Einstein responded with the words "Whatever scientific phenomenon you have discovered requires proof, either mathematical or physical, if any scientist is to investigate."

I was just about to read the third letter, curious to find out what Weldon eventually said to get Einstein to visit, when I heard footsteps.

It was hard to tell where they were coming from, but it wasn't hard to tell that they were moving quickly.

"Time to cruise," Eddie said.

I forced myself to heed the warning I'd given Eddie about taking memorabilia and stuck the precious letters back in the drawer. Then I headed for the window.

Eddie headed for the door.

"Where are you going?" I said.

"To the basement."

"Going through the portal without knowing what the hell we're doing is a mistake."

The footsteps were louder and closer now. There was no time to argue. I opened the window, ready to climb out, and Eddie opened the study door, ready to run out, but neither of us ended up going anywhere—

Van Doran stepped into the study. "You gentlemen are in way over your heads."

"That's right," I said. "We are. So why don't you fill us in?"

"You know too much already."

"We don't know anything. That's why we're here. To find some answers." I glanced at the blackboard of equations. Van Doran motioned to it and laughed.

"You want to ask him yourself?"

"You mean Einstein?"

"Who else would I mean? Maybe you can get him to confess his precious secret in person."

My heart started racing wildly. Was he joking? Would my twelve-year quest lead to a direct conversation with Einstein, in person, *alive*?

I glanced at Eddie. There was a mixture of disbelief and dread on his face. "You sure that's a good idea?" he said, and he wasn't asking Van Doran. He was asking me.

And I guess he was thinking the same thing I was. *Oh, the things that could go wrong in this scenario.*

Van Doran backed out into the hallway. "Albert! I found what you're looking for."

After a few seconds of silence, I heard approaching voices.

Van Doran turned toward them. "When it comes to reasons why we need to make progress faster, I've found Exhibit A, Albert." He motioned into the room, indicating that we were Exhibit A. "If we don't move faster, problems like this will multiply."

Einstein stepped into the room after him, and this time my impression of the scientist was completely different than it had been the day before. Seeing him across the lawn had been like seeing him across the span of history—a faraway figure, an untouchable icon.

But up close, he was a flesh-and-blood man with sagging jowls, deep-set, rheumy eyes, and gray, unkempt hair. He didn't look well, and I immediately realized this was because of his surgery and his aortic aneurism. His bad health had taken its toll.

Eddie and I were glued to the man, and what happened next was the least understandable and most horrific part of this nightmarish journey.

Van Doran stepped back into the room, pulled out a handgun, and, without so much as a hitch in his motion, shot Einstein in the back of the head—

There was a sudden burst of blood and flesh, and Einstein collapsed to the floor.

I was numb with shock. Eddie was frozen in disbelief.

Dark burgundy blood pooled around Einstein's head and his unkempt gray hair started soaking it up, turning the gray plum red.

I was beyond thinking this nightmare was some kind of hallucination, but right then, it seemed that it had to be. This was too impossible to be reality.

Einstein had just been murdered.

Surely Van Doran would gun me and Eddie down next, so I told myself to make a run for it, but right then Clavin ran into the room.

He took one look at the horror in front of him and shouted at Van Doran, "What in God's name have you done?"

"If he dies now, instead of in the hospital, he can't write his deathbed confession."

"What deathbed confession?"

Clavin hasn't time traveled, I thought, but before I could process the implications of that, Van Doran shot Clavin in the chest.

Clavin's body reared back, and Van Doran shot him again. Clavin crumpled to the floor, blood blooming through his shirt.

Eddie must've anticipated that we were slated to be next because he was already three quarters of the way across the study when Van Doran wheeled back toward us—

Eddie slammed into him, sending him flying into the wall and down hard. I didn't need to be prompted and was already following Eddie out into the hallway. History was repeating itself, but this getaway was much cleaner and faster.

As we ran down the hallway toward the kitchen, I didn't try and talk Eddie out of using the portal. Under these conditions, it was the best escape route.

We sprinted into the kitchen and down into the basement. Eddie raced toward the wall, and as he went through, my strong reservations about using the portal again swept over me. We hadn't found any answers, only more questions, and things had gotten worse. Much worse.

And that was the thought that carried me through the wall.

Chapter Fifteen

The white ocean surrounded me, and the heat was suffocating. I continued running until the oxygen disappeared, then I bent over and tried to suck in air. After a minute or so, I was able to catch my breath. The oxygen had returned to the room.

I used my shirt to wipe the sweat from my face as I checked my surroundings. Stone walls, a desk, and bookcases.

I was back in Alex's carrel.

Then two things hit me simultaneously. Eddie wasn't here, and though the furniture in Alex's carrel was the same, Alex's stuff was gone. The room was barren. As if Alex had moved out, or hadn't moved in yet.

And what about Eddie? Where was he? The obvious guess was that he'd traveled to a different time period than I had, and wouldn't that be just dandy. It would add another wild card to an increasingly chaotic distortion of history.

I looked back at the wall through which I'd arrived, and this time I saw it for what it was. Not a weird portal, but a wormhole. An Einstein-Rosen bridge. Theories postulated that it could exist, and those theories had turned out to be right.

With that one question answered, though the answer didn't help me at all, I unlocked the carrel door, and stepped out into the tunnel.

The tunnel hadn't changed. It was still dimly lit and unmarked. Using Alex's key, which I still had, I locked the door behind me, and hoped my sense of direction would carry me to the trap door.

As I swung down tunnel after tunnel, I was reminded of the multiple-timeline theory of time travel. It was a messy theory, but at least it allowed for all histories to exist. One where Alex lived, and one where Alex died. The time travel that I was living through seemed far messier than this model or any of the other models. Anything could happen at any time. History was in flux.

That meant I had to double down on the history I knew. Time was counting on me forgetting, so I had to count on remembering.

Soon after that thought, I saw light spilling out from an open carrel up ahead. So far, I'd been lucky. I hadn't run into anyone, nor passed an open carrel, so no one had called me out as a trespasser.

I thought about doubling back rather than risk walking by the open carrel, but decided to forge ahead. My sense told me that I was finally moving in the right direction.

I moved past the open carrel, when a woman's voice called out, "Jacob?"

That didn't stop me, even though I thought I recognized the voice.

"Jacob?" The woman had stepped out into the tunnel.

I glanced back and saw that it was Laura. Her short red hair was mussed and her hazel eyes seemed more golden in the dim light. I fell for her all over again.

"Oh… hi…" I said, rapidly processing how it was possible that we knew each other. I must've returned to some time after we'd had our first "date" on Jackson Hill. "Do you have a carrel down here?"

She shook her head. "I'm visiting a friend."

"Invite him in here," said a woman's voice from inside the carrel.

Synchronicity was hard at work again. It had put Laura right in my path, even though she didn't have a carrel down here. It was the vortex of Einstein's secret, attracting everything it needed into its powerful orbit, changing facts and history as it pleased.

Laura motioned for me to enter the carrel, then introduced me to Mila, a lanky brunette with a gracious smile. "Jacob was a good friend of Alex's from college. We met at Alex's memorial service."

The permutations zipped through my mind. Laura had met me at the memorial, so Alex had already been murdered. I'd traveled to the right era, but had arrived a little too late.

"I'm sorry," Mila said. "He was a great guy."

And I didn't come back early enough to save him. "It's still hard to believe he's gone," I said.

There was an awkward silence until Mila filled it with the question that I'd been dreading. "Hey, how'd you get in here?"

"I came down with Eddie, and I got lost on the way back from the bathroom." Hopefully, I hadn't flubbed it and Eddie still had a carrel down here.

"Well, you took a wrong turn," Mila said. "Three, in fact."

"Can you set me back on course?" Now that I'd avoided one pitfall, I was ready to get out.

"Go left, then take the second right."

"Thanks." I started toward the door.

"Can I talk to you for a second?" Laura asked.

Apparently, synchronicity wasn't going to let up. "Sure."

She stepped out into the tunnel and I followed. Once we were out of earshot of Mila, Laura spoke. "Why are you here?"

"I told you. Eddie invited me."

"I don't mean down here. Why'd you come back to UVA?"

Come back? Again, I had to quickly calculate the permutations. She wouldn't have asked me this unless I'd already left town after the memorial.

"I—ah—I'm interviewing for a job," I said. *Stupid!* I didn't even know if there was an opening.

"What job?"

"There's an opening in the School of Education, to help administer a Science Foundation grant." At least I didn't say a job in the history department, her area of expertise.

"That's kind of what you do at USC."

"But better." I smiled, trying to act confident with my lies.

"Why did Eddie bring you down to the Caves?" She was relentless.

"Are you interrogating me?"

"Not exactly. But when I saw you, I..." Her aggressiveness was dissipating. "Well, I'm not sure how to put it. It kind of fit in."

"I'm not following you." But I *was* following. It did fit in. The question was: *How the hell did she know it fit in?*

"Of course, you're not following me," she said. "I need to explain a couple of things first. I have a class in thirty minutes. How about we meet at Greenley's after that?"

"Sure." If she had a class, that meant she'd decided to go to law school after all. "What class?"

"5055. It's an introductory survey course." I tried not to let her see my shock. She wasn't going to law school. She was teaching one of the courses I was supposed to teach. But she wasn't filling in for me. "You're filling in for Alex."

She lowered her eyes. "Yeah. Not the way I wanted to get an appointment. But there you have it." Her lip quivered a bit, betraying the guilt she felt for landing her dream job through someone else's tragedy.

Laura hadn't killed for the job. Van Doran had done the killing for her.

"Let's say four o'clock," she said.

"See you then."

She headed back to Mila's carrel, and I was left, once again, with the task of finding the trap door. Why didn't synchronicity help out with some of these more practical matters?

A few minutes later, it did help out. I turned down a tunnel and saw those carved slots in the wall. I hurried over to them, climbed up, and pushed the trap door open.

*

Before stepping out of Grace Hall, I picked up a campus paper from a stack by the door and checked the date. *September 15.*

So I'd traveled into the future this time. Not by much. It was a couple of weeks after my visit to Clavin in the hospital. The academic year had started, and I'd already been fired from my appointment.

No—that wasn't right. In this version of history, Laura had landed the coveted faculty appointment. So I probably hadn't flown out to UVA for an interview. Instead, I'd flown out for Alex's memorial.

The small trails blazing into history were drastically changing facts. I was tempted to call myself in L.A. and ask myself a boatload of questions to find out exactly just how much had changed.

But I resisted and stepped outside. The fresh air felt good, and the normalcy of the campus was calming. I asked a passing student for the time, and found I still had a few hours before my meeting with Laura. So there was plenty of time to research other changes. Primarily Einstein's murder. Was that a fact now? If it was, that meant I'd have to resurrect both Alex and Einstein. *And* Clavin. Did Einstein's secret even still exist as a historical fact? It was possible that it had all changed.

I pulled out Alex's iPhone to start the search, but the SIM card didn't work, which made sense considering it was nine months after Alex's death.

So my task was to get to a computer. I considered going to Eddie's, but teaming up with him again seemed more than stupid. The first time I'd teamed up with him, it had ended with Alex dead. The second time, with Einstein dead. Maybe the key was to avoid Eddie completely.

I still had my faculty ID card, so I headed over to Alderman Library. The card got me into the library—all I had to do was flash it in front of the security guard—but it wasn't going to get me onto a computer terminal. I was no longer a faculty member. If I tried to log in, the system wouldn't recognize my ID number.

Fortunately, the library offered one-day guest passes. I went to the service desk, filled out a form—which probably blazed its own trail into history—then found an available terminal and went to work.

First up was Einstein. It didn't take more than thirty seconds to discover that a new history had established itself. Over sixty years ago, Einstein had disappeared without a trace. There was no mention of murder. I read through a number of biographical summaries of Einstein's life, and they all contained the same information. The great scientist had mysteriously vanished. And, of course, this was fodder for one of the great eccentricities of American culture.

Conspiracy theories.

And I found a ton of them. Everything from alien abduction to government-sanctioned murder.

I waded through the craziness, trying to separate fact from fiction, but it was impossible. In the end, when it came to this version of history, there was only one fact that I was sure was real. I had witnessed that fact myself.

Van Doran had murdered Einstein.

I did find a quote from Ruth Meyer, Einstein's personal assistant, which hinted at this truth. She had told authorities that Einstein had left for a two-day private conference and never returned. She was right. That "conference" was the visit to Weldon's estate.

Next, I moved on to something that I wasn't too keen on checking. I still clung to the hope that, even with all the other changes, the key component that defined the old history had somehow remained intact. The pit of my stomach tightened as I searched the *Trenton Evening Times* for the article that had launched my twelve-year quest. The article where Nurse Ander had said that Einstein's last words in German might be the same words he'd written on those pages next to his bed.

The article didn't exist. Which meant Einstein had never written that confession. Which meant there was no secret.

But just to confirm that the new history had wiped out all traces of the secret, I also searched for the *Fame* article. It no longer existed either.

The secret, the key to understanding everything and fixing anything, was gone. Just like Mr. Gregory Van Doran wanted.

But *I* was still here. He hadn't gotten rid of me. Yet. And he wouldn't even have to get rid of me if my doubts grew. I had to cling to the correct history whether the facts still existed or not. I had to fight the doubts about which history was the correct history. I had to fight reconstructed memories.

Alex had started me on the quest, and he was dead.

No… Alex had *not* started me on the quest.

Or had he?

It was the *Trenton Evening Times*. It was *Fame* magazine. I had to remember those facts.

But doubt slid in among those facts. There was no article quoting Nurse Ander. Einstein clearly hadn't died in Princeton Hospital.

Was Alex why I'd pursued Einstein's confession? Had he gone back in time and started me down this path?

I suddenly had a clear memory of that.

During my sophomore year, when I'd ventured out to that yard sale in search of a lamp for my dorm room, he'd come with me. He was the one who'd led me over to that box of magazines, the box that had yielded the *Fame* magazine.

Right then, in Alderman Library, in front of that computer terminal, I saw that memory clearly, not aware in the least that I might be a victim of a reconstructed memory.

You see, how could I be aware? It was just as possible that my other memory of that yard sale, the one without Alex, the one where I'd discovered the magazine on my own, could've been the reconstructed memory.

My next move was to check and see if Einstein's "disappearance" had sent ripples throughout this new history. I leapt from one well-known event to another, skimming broad swaths of history after Einstein's disappearance. The Kennedy assassination, the moon landing, the Vietnam War, Watergate, the Iranian hostage crisis, *Gore v. Bush*, 9/11, the Iraq War, the election of Obama.

I couldn't find one change in any of those major events.

Then I checked for changes in the corner of history that I knew so well, the history of science, sticking to the period after Einstein's disappearance. I went through everything from the Mercury space program to the launch of the Hubble Space Telescope to the emergence of string theory. Nothing had changed.

The only parts of history that had changed dealt with Einstein's confession—and, as I was beginning to understand, with the lives of those involved in that confession. Einstein, Clavin, Eddie, Van Doran, Weldon, Alex, and me.

And that confession now existed in only one place. At the intersection of those lives.

Then I realized that someone else's life might be involved. Laura's life. She'd said that seeing me "fit in" with something. I had a hunch it fit in with Einstein. For her sake, I hoped it didn't.

Chapter Sixteen

I arrived at Greenley's early. The patrons were boisterous, and I took that to mean the excitement of the new semester was still in play.

I ordered my coffee, found a seat in the back, and pondered how changes in history could be so isolated.

Of course, I didn't come up with an answer, but this phenomenon did kill off another time-travel trope. There was no huge "butterfly effect" to time travel. If one event changed, it didn't have millions of repercussions. And that must've somehow been connected to synchronicity. Time travel affected only those who came into contact with that one event.

As I was trying to wrap my head around that and figure out exactly what that meant, Laura, coffee in hand, sat down in front of me.

"You never told me why Eddie invited you down to the Caves," she said, starting right back in with the interrogation.

"Einstein," I said, deciding not to hedge my answers unless I had to get into time travel. "He wanted to show me a document that might help with my research."

"I thought you said you were abandoning that?"

I must've have told her that during my visit here for Alex's memorial service. Exactly how much had I told her?

"I tried to give it up," I said. "But that didn't work out so well."

She took a sip of her coffee, and I waited for her next question. But she shifted gears. "This is going to sound kind of weird."

"Try me."

"Okay… But I need to ease you into it… After the memorial, I was in a fog," she said. "I hadn't been close to Alex, but it still hit me hard. No way as hard as it hit you, and some of his students, but hard enough that it was on my mind all the time. That might've been because of our hike up Jackson Hill. You said a lot of things up there that made me feel close to Alex, closer than I'd been to him when he was alive."

So I'd gone to Jackson Hill with her in this version of history, too. A fact that hadn't changed, no butterfly effect, and I wondered if that meant anything.

"After a few weeks, I finally started to get back to normal. I didn't think about it all the time and the newspapers stopped speculating about the hit-and-run. But I noticed Eddie was acting weird, and unlike Alex, I knew Eddie well. After Alex died, Eddie wasn't as friendly anymore. He was kind of somber, like he was worried about something. He started to avoid me.

"Then I heard a rumor that the police had talked to him after the hit-and-run. So I started to wonder if Eddie had been involved in Alex's death. I know that's an awful thing to think, but I couldn't help it. I tried to talk to him a few times, to convince myself that he was the same old Eddie, and that he wasn't hiding something, but each time I talked to him he found some way to cut the conversation short. That made me more suspicious.

"So I checked out the rumor, and it turned out that the police *had* talked to Eddie. It also turned out that some of his other friends thought he'd become more reclusive. So it wasn't just me. And then Mila told me something strange.

"Eddie had asked the Cabal if he could transfer carrels. He wanted Alex's carrel."

I tried not to betray that I was spooked. Her description of what was going on with Eddie was also a perfect account of Einstein's final months. The change in demeanor, the growing somberness, *and* the suspicion that he was hiding something. The parallel signaled to me that Eddie, *this* Eddie, like Einstein, knew something about time travel. That's what he was hiding.

"Are you saying you think Eddie killed Alex? For his carrel?"

"No—that's crazy. But there's one more thing that I haven't told you."

"What is it?"

Her eyes went wide and she looked frightened. "I have to show it to you. It's on Jackson Hill."

"How does it tie in with Eddie?"

"When I asked him to take a look at it, he stopped talking to me altogether. That's how."

*

We drove out of Charlottesville in her car. The first time I'd driven to Jackson Hill, I'd had only one thing on my mind. Her. Hoping we'd hit it off. This time, I was focused on Van Doran. I kept checking the side-view mirror to see if he was following us.

"You're awfully nervous," she said.

"I haven't been getting much sleep lately."

"You worried about the job interview?"

"Among other things."

She flashed a sympathetic smile.

I didn't want to get into an extended conversation, so I didn't say anything more. I was worried that I'd contradict something the "other" me had said to her when he'd come to Charlottesville.

She made some attempts at small talk, but my reticence eventually won the day and she stopped. About thirty minutes later, we pulled into the parking lot at the base of Jackson Hill.

"We're going up to Gray's Cabin," she said.

I wasn't surprised.

As we hiked up, I racked my brains trying to figure out how Gray's Cabin could be connected to Eddie, to time travel, or to Einstein's secret.

Could it be another time-travel portal?

Laura's pace up the trail was fast. Much faster than on our last hike. She was focused on her destination, which was fine by me.

When we reached the cabin, she marched right in without saying a word. But just before I followed her inside, I thought I saw movement in the woods. I told myself it was either my growing paranoia or an animal shuffling by. I should've known better.

Laura flicked on the light, and I took in the cot, the metal plates, the pot, the iron skillet, the wood-burning stove, and the display case. Everything looked exactly as it had before.

"I don't know how or when it changed," she said.

I scanned the place more carefully, but still didn't see any changes. Of course, I didn't know the place as well as she did.

She headed over to the display case. "Take a look in here."

I walked over and did just that. My eyes ticked over Corbin's books. Thoreau, Emerson, Fuller, and Whitman. Plus the magazine with a write-up on Corbin's adventure—

And that's where I saw the change.

There was a glossy magazine in there, all right, but it was no longer the *Life* magazine with Dwight D. Eisenhower on the cover. It was a *Fame* magazine, the one with a photo of Einstein on the cover, the one I knew so well. And it still teased a story on Einstein, but that story was no longer about his death and how he'd been just a regular Joe. It was about his disappearance.

I have to read this, right now, I thought. *That's why I'm here.* Just as my quest in the old history had been fueled by a clue buried in a *Fame* magazine, I was sure that this *Fame* magazine contained a clue in *this* history.

But why was this magazine here in Gray's Cabin? The *Life* magazine had been here because it contained an article on Corbin Gray.

I examined the *Fame* cover more closely and found my answer. One of the three articles teased on the cover was titled "Meet the Mountain Man."

"Do you remember what was there before?" Laura asked.

"It was a *Life* magazine."

"I don't know when it changed, but it had to be over the last month. I didn't drop in for most of August because I was busy preparing for classes. But when I hiked up this week, I saw it."

I could've told her exactly when it'd changed. In the last few days of August, when Eddie and I had traveled through the wormhole, and whatever Alex had started went from bad to worse.

"Do you think Eddie changed it?" she said.

It wasn't Eddie who had changed it. History had changed it. To "fit in."

The real question was: why had *she* noticed it?

She shouldn't have noticed the changes. The trails that a new history blazed into the old history should've been invisible to her.

And even if she did notice them, she should've blamed the changes on her faulty memory and dismissed them. That's how this works.

But she didn't dismiss it. Why?

It took me just another second to come up with the reason. It was the same reason that Eddie had noticed the changes. She'd been sucked into the vortex. Had Eddie sucked her in? Had Alex?

Had I?

She'd said that I'd spoken to her about my Einstein research during the memorial service. Not the "me" that was standing here now, but me nonetheless.

"Did you tell anyone else about this?" I asked.

"I was going to tell Mila, and take her up here this weekend, but now I don't have to. You're the person who needed to see this." She looked at the magazine, took a breath, and turned to me. "So what does it mean?"

I couldn't tell her what it meant without telling her the entire story, and that meant sucking her into the vortex even more. Van Doran would kill her just as surely as he'd killed Alex. So telling her the truth was handing her a death sentence.

And that led to a worse possibility. Was she already in danger? Had she already crossed over into knowing too much?

Dread coursed through me. "I don't know what it means," I said.

"You don't know? Or you won't tell me?"

"I don't know."

"Do you know who changed the magazine?"

"Let's go." I wanted to get her out of here and as far away from the vortex as possible. There was always the hope that her memories would change and Van Doran wouldn't have to go after her. She'd forget the old history and live in the new one.

At the same time, I also had a very selfish motive for getting her out. I wanted to come back here, alone, break into that case, and read that article. The clue to resurrecting Einstein's secret was in there.

I headed out of the cabin, hoping she'd follow.

She did. "Who changed the magazine?" she asked, again.

"I don't know."

"I don't believe you, and I think you know a lot more than you're saying."

The vortex was getting stronger.

I started down the trail. "This isn't that big of a deal." I was hoping I sounded calm enough to cover up my blatant lie. "I'm sure it's just some kind of prank."

"Why on earth would someone pull a prank like that? And why does it involve Einstein? Which means it involves you somehow."

We were out of the sight of the cabin. "I have to go to the bathroom. Go ahead and keep hiking and I'll catch up."

"Sounds like you're avoiding my interrogation," she said, and moved past me. "I'll go slow."

Not too *slow*, I thought, and not because I was avoiding her interrogation, but because I was planning to haul ass back to the cabin and get that magazine.

As I headed into the woods, I watched her move down the trail. When she was out of sight, I raced through the woods, back to the cabin.

I stepped inside and went straight for the iron skillet, but it wouldn't come off the counter. It was glued down, as it would be in any exhibit. Of course; I hadn't thought of that. I tugged hard at the handle, but the skillet wouldn't budge. There wasn't any time to mess around, so I jumped up on the counter and kicked the skillet hard.

It budged.

I kicked it again, and it flew off the counter and onto the floor.

I jumped off the counter, scooped it up, raced over to the display case, and smashed the glass with the skillet—shattering it into big chunks on the first hit.

In one swift motion, I reached inside, grabbed the magazine, and tucked it into the back of my pants, under my shirt. But that made way too big of a bulge. Laura would surely spot that I had something back there.

So I pulled it out and tucked it into the front of my pants, down around my thigh, and started toward the door. But my gait was awkward, and she'd pick up on that, too.

I pulled the magazine out again, and considered ripping the Einstein article out. But what if the clue wasn't in that article? What if it was in the article on Corbin?

There was no time to weigh all the possibilities. Laura was probably already wondering what was taking me so long. I opened the magazine, found the article, and ripped those five pages out.

I folded them, slipped them into my pocket, started toward the door and—

Stopped cold.

Laura was in the doorway. "What the hell are you doing?"

I didn't have a ready answer.

She stepped inside. "What's so critical about that magazine that you snuck back in here and destroyed my display to get to it?"

"I can't tell you." *Because the vortex will kill you.*

"Why not?"

"It has nothing to do with you."

She motioned to the case. "It does now."

"I was stupid to do that."

"No, you *had* to do it. Why?"

"Let's just go." I moved toward the door.

She slammed it shut. "I know you didn't come back to Charlottesville for a job interview. There isn't a job opening at the Ed School."

"I can't talk about this now. "

"When I saw you in the Caves, you said you were visiting Eddie. Well, I checked on that, too. Eddie wasn't down there."

"Let's just go." Again I made a move toward the door, but she stood in front of it.

"Tell me what's going on." This time, there was a hint of desperation in her voice, and that's what tipped me off. She was pressing me because she was frightened. Frightened of something more than the magazine.

And in that moment, we both looked down to the floor, where liquid was flooding into the cabin from under the door. The smell was unmistakable. It was gasoline.

Laura tried to open the door, but it wouldn't move.

I raced over and pushed on it. It was sealed shut. My heart sank as I realized I *had* seen someone out there, but had fallen into his trap anyway. And there was no doubt whose trap this was.

The gasoline was pouring into the cabin, soaking our shoes. "Move to the dry part of the floor," I said, as I lowered my shoulder and rammed the door. It didn't give an inch.

I moved over to Laura, and we both took our shoes off and tossed them back to the wet side of the cabin. But the gasoline was quickly making its way toward us, spreading smoothly in all directions.

We jumped onto the cot. I reached out to the wall to keep my balance, and felt heat emanating from the other side.

"The entire place is on fire," I said, and saw that flames were now rolling inside from underneath the door.

Laura jumped off the cot and ran to the counter, splashing through the gasoline in her bare feet.

"What are you doing?"

"Trying to save us," she said. "Get over here." She jumped onto the counter.

The flames were sweeping across the floor, and I wondered why taking refuge over there was any better than it was over here. But she knew this cabin better than anyone, so I jumped off the cot, barely outran the tide of flames sweeping across the floor, and jumped onto the counter. "What's over here?"

She moved across the counter and stepped onto the wood stove. "The stove originally had a pipe going up through the ceiling. I took it out because animals climbed in during the winter. "

In the beamed ceiling I saw a small area, about a foot and a half square, which had been patched from the outside with a board. Laura smacked the board hard, but it didn't give way. "I nailed it down pretty well and sealed it with epoxy," she said.

The cot suddenly caught fire and the old mattress instantly burst into flames. A thick, gray smoke began to fill the room.

I stepped on the stove and pounded on the board with Laura. But it was epoxied solidly into place.

I jumped back onto the countertop, bent down, and pulled at the knife that was glued to the counter. Laura was now coughing, and the cabin's wooden floor itself had caught fire, not just the gasoline.

The knife wouldn't come loose, so finally I stood up and kicked down on it, hard. That loosened it enough to wrench it free. I handed it to Laura and motioned at the board. "Pry it off."

While she tried to jam the knife into the space between the board and the ceiling, I kicked at one of the metal plates until it loosened. Then I grabbed it and joined her on the stove.

Coughing and sweating, I tried to squeeze the plate under another side of the board, but the plate was too thick to fit.

Then, as the dark smoke thickened around us, her side creaked and the board rose the tiniest fraction of an inch. I wheeled around and jammed the plate in there, and the board creaked up a little more.

We were now both coughing in spasms, but pressed on. She jammed the knife under another part of the board while I toggled the plate up and down. The board moved up a little farther, exposing the nails that ran down that side.

I started pounding on the board, and she joined in.

As the flames rose up to our feet, two more sides of the board started to give way. Desperate, and choking on the thick smoke, we pounded on the board as if we'd been buried alive—

It suddenly popped free of the nails.

Outside, I could see flames rising up from the sides of the cabin.

We were headed from the frying pan into the fire— literally— but the fire was our best hope.

I cupped my hands. "Go ahead."

She stepped up into my hands, grabbed my shoulders, and popped her head up through the opening. Then she quickly seized the edges of the opening and struggled to haul herself up. I gave her a boost and, though it was a tight fit—her arms, shoulders and hips all scraped against the edges of the opening—she made it out.

She reached down to help me.

"Go on," I said, ignoring her outstretched hands. I grabbed the edge of the opening and started to haul myself up, but the opening was so small I couldn't get any leverage. I did get high enough to see the huge flames licking up from the sides of the cabin. "Go, please!" I said.

Laura moved back, but didn't take off.

I was straining to pull the rest of my body out when she reached down into the cabin, grabbed me under my shoulders, and pulled hard, scraping more skin off her arms—

That was just enough lift to give me the leverage I needed, and I pushed off the edges and twisted myself up and out.

We both raced across the roof to the side of the cabin. Every side had flames spiking three or four feet high above the roof. Jumping through them to the ground below—about a twelve-foot drop—was the last hurdle.

"You ready?" I said.

She ran to the backside of the cabin. "The ground over here is sloped. It's less of a jump—"

She didn't hesitate, and jumped right through the flames.

I ran over and followed her down, hitting the ground hard.

As soon as the impact finished rattling my bones, I heard Laura groaning. She was holding her leg, dragging herself away from the heat of the burning cabin. Her teeth were clenched.

I scrambled over to her, and as I did, she tried to stand up, but fell back down. She couldn't put any weight on her right leg.

"Is someone trying to kill you?" she asked.

"We need to get you to a hospital."

"So you're still not going to answer my questions?" She tried to stand up again, hopping up onto one leg, but as soon as her other leg touched the ground, she grunted in pain and fell back down.

I kneeled down to her. "Give me your cell. I'll call an ambulance."

"There's no reception up here."

"Then we're going to have to get you down the trail. I can't leave you alone while I go for an ambulance." I reached for her, and she latched onto me and stood up. Then, with her leaning on me, keeping her bad leg up, I started around the cabin.

"I was almost fried alive, and you can't even tell me why," she said.

Again, that feeling of dread washed over me. Was Van Doran after me, her, or both of us? It was now clear that she, too, recognized the small trails that the new history was blazing through the old.

"I'm so sorry," I blurted out. Why hadn't her memories reconstructed themselves?

"Me too," she said, staring at the raging fire that was once her cabin. "This is connected to Alex, too, isn't it? That wasn't just a random hit-and-run."

If she's already a target, why not tell her everything? I thought.

"And this wasn't just a random arsonist?" she said.

"Let's get to the car."

We started down the trail.

It was an odd feeling to hold her so close to me, yet not tell her a word of the truth. But I held tough. I wouldn't tell her the truth unless I knew for sure that Van Doran had already targeted her. I wasn't going to be the one handing her a death sentence.

My resolve must've been palpable, because although she clung tight to me, she didn't ask me any more questions. When we hit the steepest part of the trail, she grunted and winced as the pain from her leg worsened. I felt her body quiver, ready to collapse, and held on to her more tightly.

We made it to the car, where I helped her into the passenger seat then got behind the wheel. She handed me her keys and said, "Is there something you know that's worth dying for?"

I keyed the ignition. "Don't pursue this. You're teaching at UVA. It's your dream job come true. Focus on that." I recognized that advice immediately. It was the advice that I hadn't heeded.

She didn't respond.

The trip to the hospital was a silent one.

I sat with her in the waiting room, even though she asked me to leave. As we waited, I wanted to pull out the *Fame* article. It felt heavy in my pocket, weighted with information that I desperately needed to know. Information that could save both of us.

After about thirty minutes, an orderly came out with a wheelchair, and I helped Laura into it. Then I leaned down, kissed her on the cheek, and whispered into her ear, "I promise I'll tell you everything when it's safe."

I hoped I'd never have to tell her anything at all. I hoped I could fix the changes in history, go back to my time, and continue falling in love with the beautiful Laura Metcalf, the Laura who'd never known anything about this, and who'd never been swept up into the vortex.

The orderly wheeled her away, and I walked out, more in love with her now than I'd been before.

Chapter Seventeen

I headed across the UVA Hospital grounds, on the lookout for a place to sit down so I could dive into the *Fame* article. I had regrets about leaving Laura's side, but rationalized them by convincing myself that the arsonist—and, again, I had no doubt it was Van Doran—was after me and not her.

Before I got to Jefferson Park Avenue, I spotted a bench, sat down, and pulled out the *Fame* article. I pushed away my guilt about leaving Laura and started reading.

The first few paragraphs were a quick summary of the facts, as they were known in the months following Einstein's disappearance.

Einstein had left for a private conference on Friday. A driver was to bring him back to his home on Sunday at five p.m. At seven, Ruth Meyer reported Einstein missing. But the police weren't concerned yet.

In a time when communication wasn't instantaneous, it was possible, if not likely, that the only problem was that Einstein was late.

Still, Ruth was worried. Einstein had been secretive about his whereabouts and he hadn't left her any contact information. She wasn't pleased that he'd left her in the dark. By ten o'clock that night, she was positive that something had gone wrong, and by the morning of the following day, the New Jersey State Police and the FBI were investigating.

Because this article was fresh, just a few months after the disappearance, what followed wasn't laden with conspiracy theories like the ones I'd read during my Internet search. The reporter came up with a theory, based on real facts, as to where Einstein had gone for this two-day conference.

First, without naming his source—though it was most likely Ruth Meyer herself—the reporter stated that a car with Maryland plates had picked up Einstein. Then the reporter deduced that Einstein would not have gone farther south than Washington, D.C. for any type of conference. He noted that during all the time that Einstein had lived in Princeton, the scientist had never traveled for his work farther south than D.C.

Then the reporter looked into whether there'd been a science-related conference, during the time of the disappearance, either in Baltimore or Washington, D.C.—or anywhere in between. The Maryland plates would fit in with that scenario.

But there hadn't been any public conference. So the reporter determined that it had been a private meeting. He then explored why such a meeting would be secretive.

Now, this was during the Cold War, so the reporter spoke to other scientists about new technologies that might strengthen the U.S.'s offensive and defensive capabilities. The reporter tried to connect Einstein to some of those technologies, but, in the end, he couldn't.

Then he looked into Einstein's primary research passion, his "unified field theory." Was it possible that the scientist had made a big leap, and that this leap had led to a practical application so powerful that it was being kept under wraps? The reporter reached out to Pentagon and DoD sources, but came up empty.

Then he researched the universities that Einstein might have visited on this trip. The University of Maryland, Johns Hopkins, Georgetown, Howard, and George Washington, among others. And this led him to a professor of theoretical physics at Johns Hopkins.

At this point in the article, I was convinced that the reporter was pursuing a dead end. He was far from uncovering the murder at the Weldon estate, so I started to read at a faster clip, hoping to strike gold in the next section of the article.

But while I was rushing through a description of the Hopkins professor's area of expertise, and how it connected to Einstein, I saw that this professor had a research partner, a Professor Marcus.

At UVA.

My heart started pumping faster. Surely this wasn't a coincidence. This was the clue. I had to get to a public computer terminal as fast as possible and look up Professor Marcus. First, I forced myself to read through the rest of the article, just to verify that there were no other coincidences. There weren't.

Twenty minutes later, I was sitting in front of a computer terminal in the Claude Moore Health Sciences Library. I looked up Professor Marcus and found that he'd been a professor in the School of Engineering and Applied Science at UVA in the fifties and sixties.

I found one of his journal articles, and it linked to his bio. I scanned through his bio until I found exactly what I was sure I was supposed to find. My pulse quickened and my breathing stopped. Synchronicity, history, whatever you wanted to call it—it had reached out to me again.

Professor Marcus had written "Out of Time," a short story about time travel. The story had been published in *Galaxy*, a popular science-fiction magazine from the fifties. I looked up *Galaxy* on Wikipedia and found that it had published the stories of Ray Bradbury, Robert A. Heinlein, Frederik Pohl, and many other well-known science-fiction writers. That was why Marcus had listed this credit in his bio. It was a feather in his cap.

Then I started to search for the story itself. With a title like "Out of Time," it *had* to contain the clue I needed to fix everything. The original *Galaxy* magazine wasn't online though, and although the story's title was listed on various science-fiction websites, none had a copy of it.

After searching for another thirty minutes, I sat back and stared blankly at the computer screen. The only way I was going to find a copy of that story was by digging up a hard copy of that issue of *Galaxy*.

So where could I track it down? A yard sale?

Yes. The biggest yard sale in the world.

eBay.

But how was a man with no home address, traveling through time, going to buy a magazine from eBay?

I supposed it was possible. But it would involve a P.O. box number, a money order, PayPal, and waiting for it to arrive. By that time history would have changed, and I wouldn't recognize a clue if it came from Einstein himself.

For some reason I checked eBay anyway, and found the magazine. Then my eyes fell on the seller's name, and my pulse went into overdrive, taking my heart along for the ride.

Eddie's Emporium.

Eddie had a copy of that issue of Galaxy.

So it looked like I was going to be visiting him after all.

Of course, if I could get to that magazine without interacting with him, that would be the best course of action. The magazine was probably in his house or his carrel. If it was in his house, I had a chance of getting it. But if it was in his carrel, it'd be a lot tougher. I'd have to get both the combination to the trap door and the keys to his carrel.

I took a few deep breaths and tried to calm my racing heart. Time travel was messy, but the synchronicity brought a kind of order to it, even if that order was unexplainable.

I'd gone from one issue of *Fame*, to another issue of *Fame*, to an issue of *Galaxy*, as if the same note were being played again and again on different instruments. I'd gone from one Eddie, to another, and was now headed to a third. I'd gone from a memory of my dad in a movie theater to actually seeing my dad in a drive-in. I'd gone from a hospital in Rockville to another in Charlottesville, and, although I didn't know it then, I was headed to another.

*

I crossed Jefferson Park Avenue, then made my way across campus to the Corner. From there, I hopped on a bus that ran by Eddie's place. I had considered a cab, but thought I should conserve the cash I had on hand.

Staring out the bus window at the students and townsfolk moving in and out of shops, it hit me once again just how far I was from fixing anything. No one out there knew that Einstein had made a deathbed confession, and with every passing minute, any remaining trace of that event was disappearing.

The bus took me to within a half a dozen blocks of Eddie's house, and I walked the rest of the way. I approached his rundown rental and spotted two cars out front. One of them was Eddie's. So the choice was now upon me.

I could wait until Eddie left the house and try to break in, or I could step up to the door and interact with him. It turned out that the choice wasn't that hard. As I'd realized on the bus, I couldn't wait on anything. That short story could disappear, as could my memory of it, as quickly as Van Doran had gunned down Einstein. The fastest way to that story was for Eddie to lead me to it.

I walked up the path to Eddie's front door, rang the doorbell, and braced myself for meeting a third Eddie. This time, I didn't plan to fill him in on anything. If this Eddie didn't know anything about time travel, he wasn't going to hear it from me. I'd talk to him about his fifties memorabilia and work the *Galaxy* magazine into the conversation. Let him be suspicious. Just as I'd withheld information from Laura, I'd do the same with him.

The door opened to reveal Eddie, and as I soon as I saw him, I realized how hard my task was going to be. How was I going to hide my intentions from a guy who was sharper than I was?

"Hey, I'm a friend of Alex's," I said, and extended my hand.

He shook it. "Oh, right. We met at the memorial."

Great. Now I was going to have to play the same game I'd played with Laura, trying to keep my foot out of my mouth because I had no idea what the other me had told him.

"Sorry about just dropping by uninvited, but I'm in town for a job interview, and Alex's family wanted me to follow up on some stuff that was stored in the Caves."

He looked me up and down. He wasn't buying it. "You're wearing the same clothes."

Did he mean from the memorial service? I couldn't have worn jeans and a T-shirt to the service.

He started to roll up his left shirtsleeve, and as he did, I waited for him to say something. He didn't.

And I didn't volunteer a word, either.

He continued to roll his sleeve up, past his forearm and over his upper arm, where he exposed a small, thick, pink scar. It was ugly and jaggedly circular, and though it had healed, it still had a raw look.

Though I'd never seen a bullet wound, I was sure that I was staring at one now, and it crossed my mind that I was facing the original Eddie.

But that didn't calculate—the scar looked too old for that. Though it wasn't faded like an old scar, it wasn't fresh enough to have been the result of a gunshot wound from just a few days ago.

When I looked back up at Eddie, he gave me a smile and a nod of recognition. "I made it through a few minutes after you disappeared from the basement, then I passed out. When I came to, I had no idea where you were, but I was in bad shape."

I *was* facing the original Eddie. "Van Doran's shot hit you."

"Don't worry. That was nine months ago. I'm healthy as a horse now."

"What happened?"

"I was lucky—that's what happened. The shot went straight through. So as soon as I came to, I headed to the emergency room and they patched me up. But I had to stay in the hospital a couple of days to make sure there was no chance of an infection."

He backed away from the front door and waved me inside. I walked in, plopped down on the couch, and leaned back in wonder and confusion at this bizarre turn of events.

Eddie sat down in an easy chair. "While I was in the hospital, I saw on the news that Alex had been killed in a hit-and-run. I figured it had to be related to us finding the time machine—"

"You figured right. I was with him... And it's not a time machine. It's a wormhole."

"You've been doing some investigating, huh?"

"Investigating is kinda strong. More like stumbling around."

Eddie rolled down his sleeve. "I've been doing some stumbling around myself. When I got out of the hospital, I went back to my carrel and looked through all my stuff and found something really weird. Not what was there, but what *wasn't* there. Something that should've been."

"The other you, the one that was already here, didn't know anything about Einstein's confession," I said.

"Yeah. Sounds like your stumbling around paid off. That me should've already been into all of this, but he wasn't. So I decided to find him—me—and see what else had changed about him. But I couldn't track him down."

"He was with me," I said, and I had to give time, or history, or whatever it was, a hand. It had worked everything out perfectly. While this Eddie had been in the hospital, I'd already come and gone with the other Eddie.

"I thought he'd been murdered," Eddie said. "Since Alex had been killed and you'd disappeared and there was no 'other me' around, I thought I was the lone survivor. I kept thinking the police would report my death any day, and while I was waiting for that, I found that Einstein's death was gone from history. That, instead of dying, he'd disappeared without a trace in nineteen fifty-five."

"That's why you didn't use the wormhole again."

"Yeah. I knew that our one trip through had already screwed everything up—big time. But I *was* planning to use it again. Still am. Once I figure out what's going on."

"Eddie—Einstein didn't disappear. Van Doran murdered him."

Eddie cocked his head and couldn't help but smirk. "Is that part of some conspiracy theory?"

"I wish it were, but I saw it myself. Van Doran murdered him right in front of me. He's erasing Einstein's secret, piece by piece, and the only way to keep it alive is to follow those trails. They're our lifeline back."

"But they're disappearing."

Einstein's confession is the key. "I can't be sure about this," I said, "but I have a theory about why. And it explains why the version of you that was here wasn't researching Einstein. But it's going to sound like some bullshit New Age thing—"

"Hey, don't worry about that. I already believe in time travel."

I laid out my crazy theory. "I think history helps. Sure, Van Doran wipes out evidence that Einstein left a confession, but history comes along and helps. It makes everything consistent."

"And what about us?"

"I'd like to think we're the exception, but my guess is that there *are* no exceptions. Van Doran hasn't wiped us out yet and neither has history."

"Yet…"

I reached into my pocket and pulled out the folded magazine article. "Read this."

"What is it?"

"A clue to fixing everything. I found it at Gray's Cabin, through another former UVA grad student."

"Gray's Cabin? You mean you know Laura Metcalf?"

I nodded.

"We were in the history department together," Eddie said, "but how did you end up meeting her?"

"We kind of went on a date the night before we drove up to see Clavin. But I'm talking about the Laura Metcalf that's here now."

And apparently I've been on a date with this Laura, too. "She noticed one of those trails."

It took him a second to realize what that meant. "She got sucked into this."

"Because of you."

"*I* never said anything to her."

"She said you'd become a recluse and—"

"I'd become a recluse so that she wouldn't notice that I wasn't the other Eddie."

"Well, that backfired. And now I think Van Doran might be trying to kill her, too."

"So you're blaming *me* for that?"

That reminded me of what Alex had claimed. That all of this was Eddie's fault. Was it? No, it was Alex's fault. He was the one who'd led me to that yard sale all those years ago. Or had he? I wasn't sure now. But I was sure that all roads seemed to go through Eddie. After all, here I was with him, once again.

"Just read this," I said.

He read the article, and then I filled him in on the Professor Marcus connection and the short story in *Galaxy* magazine.

"That seems like a stretch," he said. "Even for me."

"Do you have the magazine?"

"Yeah. I found it at a yard sale years ago, put it up in Eddie's Emporium, but no one's ever bought it."

"Well, now you know why. It's been waiting for us." And I hoped it still was and hadn't been cleaned up by history.

Eddie went into the bedroom to get it. After a few minutes, when he still hadn't returned, I became convinced that it was gone.

Finally he walked back into the living room, holding a magazine wrapped in a plastic sleeve. "It wasn't where I'd stored it." He offered it to me. "You read it first. It's your find."

I took the magazine, slipped it out of the sleeve, and checked the table of contents. There it was: *Out Of Time*. I flipped to the story, started reading, and was hooked. The parallels to my life and my current dilemma left no doubt that I was headed in the right direction. The old history was asking me for help.

In the story, John Peary, the main character, is hiking up the Jackson Trail in the Adirondacks, wondering what to do with his life. His life hadn't quite gone the way he'd wanted.

I wasn't surprised to see "Jackson" turn up again, not to mention a guy whose life didn't go the way he'd wanted.

On the trail, John Peary passes a cave—and, curious, he decides to go inside. The cave turns out to be a portal that transports him directly into the tunnels of the New York City sewer system.

I wasn't surprised to see tunnels either.

John moves through the tunnels, searching for a way out, then gets increasingly desperate, until he comes across a metal ladder built into a wall. He climbs it, and it leads him up into a subway station. He then exits into Manhattan and begins to explore the city.

He discovers that he's traveled ten years into the past. Since the story was written in the fifties, this means he travels back to the forties. He talks to various people, including a soldier who's just come back from World War II. That soldier notices that there's something odd about John, but can't quite put his finger on it.

He tells John, "You're like the foreigners I saw when I was stationed overseas. They were like me, but completely different."

At the end of the day, after talking to a few more people, John heads back to that subway station, down into the sewers, and back to the future from whence he came.

Three weeks later, just as he's settled back into his hometown life and starts thinking about using the portal again, a large man approaches him.

The man, who introduces himself as Ben, tells John he's lost and can't get back to his original life. It turns out that Ben has traveled through the portal so many times, he has no idea what his original life is anymore. He can't keep anything straight in his mind and he needs help. He's been trying to find a time traveler who's only gone through the portal once.

If that traveler can tell him exactly what's changed, then Ben figures he can change things back, one change at a time, until he ends up back in his original life.

Unfortunately, John says, "I haven't noticed any changes in my life." But that leads him to question himself: *Were* there changes? Changes he just hadn't noticed? So he decides to go through the portal again, and this time pay closer attention to the changes when he comes back.

Bad move.

In the end, John ends up traveling through the portal so many times that he, too, can't remember which life is his original life. And during one of those trips, he runs into that soldier again. This time John tells *him* the story of the time-travel portal. It's John's desperate attempt to remember which life was his original life. The soldier doesn't believe that there's a time-travel portal, so John takes him to it.

There, the soldier decides he wants to try it. John halfheartedly warns him, and as the soldier stands on the threshold, not sure whether to try it or not, we learn why John's warning was so mild.

John is planning to wait right there until the soldier returns, and then go back out to Manhattan with him and ask him what's changed. Like Ben, John hopes that he can get back to his original life by figuring out how the changes work.

Then, just as John admits to himself that his plan is exactly the same as Ben's, and Ben's didn't work, the soldier goes through the portal.

The story ends with John realizing that the soldier could have helped him. The key was that the soldier was able to recognize John as a foreigner, a time traveler, without having to travel through time.

But it's too late now.

*

As soon as I finished reading, Eddie asked me what I'd found.

I handed it to him. "You read it before I tell you."

He started, and I ticked through the elements of the story, trying to figure out which applied and which didn't. I suspected a couple of elements might apply, while others were nothing more than parts of a science-fiction story.

I was disappointed that there wasn't a direct link to Einstein's confession. On the other hand, why should there be? So far, no clue had been direct. It was part of the messiness of time travel.

When Eddie finished the story, he said, "It seems more like a warning than a clue. If you travel through time too much, you don't know what your original life is anymore."

"It's definitely a warning. And from what I've seen so far, a totally legitimate warning. But I'm sure there's also a clue in there. Something that we're supposed to do."

"Well, let me throw something else your way," Eddie said. "Maybe you can make sense of it. I noticed it when I was looking through Alex's stuff—"

"How'd you get to look at his stuff?"

"When his parents came, they weren't too good about cleaning out his place." Knowing how little they cared about their son, that didn't surprise me. "I went through what they left behind, thinking I might find out how the portal worked. Instead, I found out who his next biography was going to be about—"

"Einstein." That piece fell into place right then.

"Yep. And he'd already done a lot of work on it. But he needed more information. So he enlisted us."

He went back to my sophomore year and took me to that yard sale. Now I was sure about that.

"From his notes," Eddie said, "I saw that he was going to focus on answering the one question that'd make his book a bestseller."

"He was going to solve the mystery of Einstein's disappearance," I said, and as soon as I'd said it, the new history fell neatly into place as naturally as if it had been the correct history all along.

Einstein had *always* disappeared, and there'd always been hundreds of theories about what had happened to him. The history with the confession was the wrong history. It was the result of too much time travel. *It* was the phony history.

I looked down at the short story in Eddie's hands, and seeing it stopped that freight train of thoughts. There was still a part of me that knew those facts were wrong. Those facts were the new facts, not the original ones.

But the new history was crushing the original one, and this short story could help the original fight back. This short story contained a clue. What *was* that clue?

"The soldier's the clue," I suddenly blurted out.

"What?"

"The soldier recognizes the time traveler, the foreigner, even though he hasn't traveled through time himself."

"And…"

"John realizes the soldier could've helped him."

"But the soldier *doesn't* help him."

"He can't. Once he goes through the portal, he's tainted. He can't help anymore."

"And how does that help *us*?"

"We need to find the soldier."

"Okay…"

"And the soldier is someone who recognizes the time traveler, or the trails—"

"But who hasn't traveled through time themselves." Eddie was catching on.

"Exactly," I said. "And there's only one person who fits the bill—Laura."

"Are you kidding? First you blame me for sucking her into this. And now you *want* to suck her into it?"

I didn't want to. But I had to.

Chapter Eighteen

I found Laura ensconced in a hospital room on the third floor. She had a fresh cast on the lower part of her leg and a frown on her face. Before I could say anything, she asked, "Are you ready to tell me what's going on?"

"It's not safe yet."

"But you need my help, don't you?"

"Yeah, I do."

"Then it sounds to me like you *can't* wait until it's safe. You're going to have put your cards on the table now."

She was right. But I'd still start slow, leaving the part about the wormhole out of the equation for now.

"There's someone out there who wants to keep something that Einstein wrote a secret. And that someone tried to kill me at the cabin."

"And what's the secret?"

"I don't know."

"Back to that again."

"No, I honestly don't know." That part was true.

"You're going to have to tell me more if you want my help."

"It'll sound ridiculous."

"That's my call, isn't it?"

As soon as she said that, I remembered the suspicion I'd had right before the fire broke out. "You've seen something ridiculous yourself." *Something that frightened you.*

"Good work, detective."

"Tell me what you saw."

"I think we were in the middle of you doing the telling."

"Okay. How's this for starters? Einstein was murdered."

"So you're a conspiracy nut? Let me guess: sixty years later, Einstein's killer is tracking you down?"

"The murder didn't happen sixty years ago."

"I was rounding off."

"I know you were. And I mean it didn't happen that way originally."

She was about to counter when a nurse came into the room. I looked at the nurse's nametag, saw that her name wasn't familiar, and felt relief. Even though I was in a hospital, again, with a patient, again, and a nurse, the coincidences stopped there.

The nurse stepped up to Laura. "How you doing, honey?"

"Pretty good."

"Good enough to fill out some paperwork?"

"Sure."

The nurse handed Laura a clipboard and pen. "I'll be back in twenty to pick it up."

She exited, and Laura reached over to the table next to her bed, opened the drawer, and pulled out her purse. She fished her wallet out of her purse, and I thought she was going take out her insurance card. Instead, she pulled out her smartphone.

"I want to show you one of my favorite pictures," she said. "It's a picture of my mom when she was a kid. It was taken in the fifties. My mom gave it to me when I was a kid, and I'd stare at it, imagining the world that she grew up in. I'd try to will myself into that world."

Laura handed me her phone and I looked at the picture. A young girl, around ten years old, was standing at a distance, smiling at the camera. Off to her left, barely in frame, was a concession stand, where a few patrons waited in line. Behind her were bloated cars, in a tidy row, with their trunks to the camera. In front of those cars were more rows of cars, leading up to the far end of the photo, which was dominated by a huge movie screen.

Laura's mom was at a drive-in theater.

I felt the blood pumping through my veins at warp speed.

"I'd imagine myself at that drive-in with my friends," Laura said. "Of course, I'd never been to a drive-in, but I thought it'd be fun to see movies there instead of at the multiplex where I usually went."

Laura stopped there, and I thought it was because she'd noticed the look of incredulity on my face. It wasn't.

"But there's something new in the picture," she said, her voice starting to tremble. "I don't know when it appeared. I mean, you know how you walk by something so many times that you don't even see it anymore? I had that picture in a frame on my sideboard, and I'd glanced at it now and then, but I hadn't really looked at it for a long, long time. And I might have never noticed a change at all, except that I got a Groupon for ninety percent off on digitizing pictures.

"So I collected some pictures, and I took that one out of the frame, and that's when I noticed it. One of the men waiting in line at the concession stand—" Laura's eyes filled with tears. "He's looking back at the camera. He was never looking back before. No one was looking at the camera except my mom."

There were four people waiting in front of the concession stand, and the second one from the front had his head turned back, looking at the camera. His face was visible, and though it wasn't in perfect focus, it was easy enough for me to recognize him.

Henry Clavin.

My stomach clenched. This was a small trail, one that only Laura, alone, could've recognized. *And* the only way it could've ever had any significance would be if she showed it to me. I was the one who knew the role that Clavin played in Einstein's confession. This photo was meant for me.

Laura was the soldier.

Clavin stared at the camera with a haunted expression on his face, as if he were looking out at me personally, pleading with me. *Can you bring me back to life?*

"You know who it is?" Laura said.

"…Yeah."

"But you don't want to tell me."

"You sure he wasn't looking at the camera before?" I knew she was sure, but I asked anyway.

"I know everything about that picture. The number of cars, where they're parked, the number of people in line, what they're wearing, every shadow and reflection, and I know that man was never looking into the camera."

"Did your mom grow up in Maryland or Pennsylvania?"

"In Maryland—how did you know?"

"That's where this man lived." I didn't want to say much more about Clavin. What I wanted to do was track him down. "Can I google something on your phone?"

She nodded, and I immediately googled Clavin.

I whipped through as much information as I could find. In this version of history, he wasn't connected to Einstein. At least, as far as I could tell from my perfunctory search. But he was similar to the Clavin that I'd left back in my original history. Though I couldn't tell if he'd lived in Princeton, New Jersey, he had definitely lived in Frostburg, Maryland, a small town fifteen miles from Cumberland.

In this version of history, he'd died in the fifties. He hadn't died in Rockville just a few weeks ago. And I knew how he'd died. Van Doran had murdered him. So what I couldn't figure out was why Clavin's death had been recorded, if he'd "disappeared" like Einstein.

After digging deeper, my question was answered by a small announcement, dated August 17, 1957, in the notices section of a Western Maryland paper. Allegany County had *declared* Henry Clavin dead. He had actually disappeared, but once the legally required amount of time had passed, the County had officially pronounced him dead.

Unlike Einstein's disappearance, Clavin's disappearance was an open-and-shut case—because no one cared to keep it open. There weren't millions of Internet pages dedicated to speculation about his disappearance.

My stomach tightened as my spirits sank. This search had literally concluded with a dead end. So why was Clavin in that photo if he was a dead end? Just as I'd resigned myself to the idea that the photo wasn't the right path to follow, I saw a weird hit on the fifth page of my Google search. A Henry Clavin, from Frostburg, Maryland, had been interviewed on a radio show.

I clicked through and found a site that had digitized a variety of radio shows from the fifties, including a show entitled *What Will Tomorrow Bring*. The show consisted of interviews with everyday folk who tried to predict what changes the future would bring.

Clavin had been a guest on one of the episodes.

I glanced up at Laura and weighed whether to play that episode in front of her.

"No comment on your research?" she said.

"I found something that I'd like to listen to. It's an interview with the man in the picture."

"You ready to tell me who he is?"

"He was a friend of Einstein's."

"So what the hell is he doing in my mom's photo?"

"I don't know."

"How many times are you going to use that line?"

"I'm hoping not many more."

"Bullshit. Why are you so afraid to tell me the whole story? Would you have to kill me if you did, like in a movie?" Her cheeks were rosy with anger. "Well, guess what? Someone already tried to kill me. That's why they waited until we were both in that cabin."

I didn't want to argue with her. Not now. "I'm in way over my head, and the only way out is to listen to this interview."

She waved her hand at me dismissively. "Then go ahead."

I clicked on the episode, which was called "Mind Over Matter," and read the description. There was nothing there that suggested a connection to Einstein, at least not that I could see. I clicked the play button.

The first interview was with a young woman who believed that in the future we'd be able to move objects with our minds. The host led her into a speculative discussion in which she theorized that someday we'd learn to control the electrons in our minds and use them like a laser tractor beam to move objects.

I skipped to the next interview. It was with a man who sounded older, much too old to be Clavin. I skipped forward again and landed in the middle of the next interview. This guest was talking about time travel. It had to be Clavin.

I skipped back until I found the beginning of the interview, then let it roll. The host introduced the guest, Henry Clavin, and bantered with him about H.G. Wells' *The Time Machine,* which Clavin had read, and then Isaac Asimov's *The End of Eternity,* which Clavin hadn't read. Then the host asked Clavin what he thought we'd be capable of controlling with our minds in the future.

Clavin said we'd be able to control time travel. It wasn't going to work with knobs and dials like a normal machine. We wouldn't be plugging in dates. Instead, we'd think about where we wanted to go and that's where we'd go.

My stomach relaxed, and I let out a deep breath. My hunch had been right. The soldier, Laura, had led me to a clue with real value. I suddenly felt elated and took a deep, deep breath. I let it out slowly.

I wanted to run out and tell Eddie that I knew how the wormhole worked. Clavin hadn't led me to Einstein's confession, but he'd put me back on the right track. When it came to using the wormhole, mind over matter was the set of instructions. And if I knew how to use the wormhole properly, I could fix all that had gone horribly wrong.

The interview ran another couple of minutes. The host asked Clavin what the time machine would look like and Clavin said he didn't know. Then the host asked him when man would invent the time machine, and Clavin's answer sent a chill down my spine.

He said, "Maybe man doesn't *invent* it, but *discovers* it." For me, this was confirmation that Clavin was guiding me in the right direction.

The host ended the interview, then started to introduce the next guest. I clicked the show off and handed the phone back to Laura.

"So this is tied to time travel?" she said.

"Yes." It was hard not to crack a smile, so I did. Not because I wanted to hide the truth, but because the only preparation she had for that truth was *What Will Tomorrow Bring*, a kitschy program from the fifties. Not quite the groundwork I wanted to lay.

"That's the best lie you could come up with," she said.

"It's not a lie."

"Do you think I'm an idiot?"

"Of course not."

"So the secret is time travel."

"Laura, how did a sixty-year-old picture of your mom suddenly change?"

"Photoshop."

"Why would someone break into your place and photoshop some random picture?"

She stared at me with hard eyes. "Occam's Razor."

Occam's Razor was a scientific principle that posited that the simplest answer was usually the right one. But Laura had made a mistake by bringing that up. This fell into my corner of history, the history of science.

"So what's the simplest answer?" I said.

She looked down at her phone and brought up the picture of her mom again. She didn't say anything for a minute or so. I guess she was weighing what the simplest answer was.

"I never noticed that this man was looking at the camera before. I must've always been too focused on my mom."

"You really believe that you missed that for all those years?"

She frowned. "Okay—then it was photoshopped. That's the simplest answer."

"Let me fill you in on Occam's Razor. It hasn't stood the test of time. It's an artifact of medieval science. The examples where it doesn't work are all over the place. From modern physics with string theory to modern biology. Hundreds of things run counter to Occam's Razor, including the complexity of DNA. And DNA is life itself."

"So you jump from photoshop to time travel?"

I smiled. "I know it sounds insane, but I can prove it. If you Skyped me in Los Angeles right now, I'd be there. Only it would be the me who belongs to this time, not the me you found in the Caves." I was sounding like a lunatic.

She shook her head, then sighed. "I think I need to get some sleep."

She was the soldier, so maybe that was a way to get her to believe me. "Laura, you felt it. You knew it. The second you saw me in the Caves, you knew I didn't belong there."

"Yeah, because you *didn't* belong there. You don't have a carrel."

"You know that's not what I'm getting at. You saw me and thought, 'He's out of place here.' You felt that so strongly that you checked to see if Eddie was down there. And you checked to see if there was a job opening."

She didn't say anything. She stared at me for a few seconds, then put her phone in her purse and put her purse back in the drawer. The anger was gone, replaced by pensiveness.

It was time to back off. "Laura, whether you believe me or not, promise me you'll be careful."

"I'll be fine. I'm not going anywhere. They're keeping me here for a couple of days."

I had no evidence to prove that Van Doran couldn't march into the hospital and execute her, but I felt that she was safe for the moment. As long as she didn't travel through the wormhole.

"I have to go," I said.

"Where?"

"Back to where I came from."

Chapter Nineteen

I went back to Eddie's place and filled him in on *What Will Tomorrow Bring*. He wasn't sold on the concept of controlling time travel with your thoughts.

"So you just have to believe, huh?"

"I'm going to sound like one of those nuts who tries to justify his crazy theory with quantum mechanics, but I'm doing it anyway."

"Desperate times call for desperate measures."

I had to smile. "One of the principles of quantum physics is that the observer affects the outcome." I'd taught that in my history of science classes. "It's worth a try." I wanted to move forward before the original version of history completely disappeared. On my way over to Eddie's, for about five minutes, I'd believed that Einstein had always disappeared.

"So you just think about where you want to go and poof, you end there? Like Dorothy with the ruby slippers."

"Except I don't have the slippers. But I do know this. The first time I went through the wormhole, I had one thought on my mind. *So this is what I do with my career opportunity at UVA.* Next thing I know I was back here during winter break, right before my big interview with McKenzie."

"How do you explain that I came back to the same time you did?"

"You followed me."

"Acceptable hypothesis, but not convincing."

"You're right, but the second trip through is the clincher. Right before I went through, I told you—the other you—that the only way to fix this is to focus on Einstein's secret. My exact words were *That's how this all started and that's the only way to fix this.*"

"And you ended up in the fifties."

"Yep, and that's where I'm going again. I'm going to go back to the weekend when Einstein was in Princeton Hospital. When he writes his confession. And I'm getting that confession before he gives it to Clavin."

I was already replaying what I knew about Einstein's last days. Mrs. Ander, the nurse who didn't know German. Dr. Dean, the doctor who gave Einstein sedatives. Ruth Meyer, Einstein's trusted assistant who was there by his side. And the papers at Einstein's bedside—

But my shoulders drooped and my momentum died when a terrible realization hit me. Those details, those facts, didn't exist anymore. That version of history had disappeared. Einstein hadn't died in Princeton Hospital.

"What's the matter?" Eddie said. "You think you need the slippers?"

"Nah—the good witch tells Dorothy that she had the power all along. But how do you travel back to a history that doesn't exist?"

"You go back to the timeline where it does exist."

"That timeline theory doesn't hold up. There's only one history."

"So every time you time travel you create a new history?"

"I don't think so. Sometimes it does and sometimes it doesn't."

"That doesn't sound very organized."

"Time travel is messy."

"Is that another one of your theories?"

"That's the one that holds up the best."

"Well, no wonder you're latching on to the Dorothy Theorem. It's a step up from 'time travel is messy.'"

"What if I told you that there was some kind of order to it, a kind of synchronicity, but I haven't figured it out?"

"I'd say we don't have the time to figure it out. We need to go through the wormhole now."

"'We? I thought you didn't believe."

"According to you, I don't have to. If I follow you through, I'm set, right?"

"So the pressure's all on me."

"Yeah, but not because of me. Because a vast chunk of history is counting on you. Not to mention Alex, Einstein, and Clavin."

*

Before we took off for the Caves, we prepared ourselves for the trip back to the fifties. This time around, we'd look like we belonged there. We changed into button-down shirts and slacks. My shirt size was the same as Eddie's, but I wasn't so lucky with the pants. They were two sizes too big for me, and when coupled with the brown Oxford shoes he lent me, which were also too big for me, I looked like a nerd.

Once we were dressed for our bizarre mission, we got online and googled maps of the Mid-Atlantic states from the fifties, then plotted our trip from Cumberland to Princeton, a four-hour drive.

"We're going to need a car to get from Weldon's Estate to Princeton," Eddie said.

"You remember that abandoned drive-in we drove by? It's not abandoned back then, so we can steal one from there." I didn't tell him that my father, as a child, worked there.

"So you've gone from being worried about breaking into a house, to stealing cars from drive-ins."

"Time travel does that to you."

He laughed.

Eddie had a few bills from the fifties in case we needed cash. He didn't deal in selling money from the fifties—there were far too many sellers of old currency to make a decent profit—but lucky for us, he'd acquired some as part of package deals with other fifties memorabilia.

We could have made more preparations, but I could feel the new history crushing my personal history. I could feel it inside myself. The correct clinical term was "reconstructing," but that didn't describe the feeling in my flesh, my bones, and my soul. There it felt like a fog was clearing to reveal a deep truth that I'd missed all my life.

I'd never seen my dad. My mom had raised me by herself. I'd always wanted to know who my dad was, but my mom had never told me. My work, the work of solving the mystery of Einstein's disappearance, had been driven by that longing to know my dad. The dad I'd never met.

That was what I felt. That reconstructed memory had pushed out the memory I'd had of my dad laughing in a movie theater. That joyous memory had become a kind of phantom image, without a basis in reality—and, sadly, without emotion.

I went through my memories of Einstein's last few days before they, too, disappeared. I didn't focus on just the last day itself.

There weren't enough details, enough facts, in the records that I'd studied, the ones that no longer existed, to feel confident enough to concentrate on that specific day. I started with the beginning of the end.

"On April thirteenth, nineteen fifty-five, Einstein didn't go to his office," I told Eddie. "He was feeling sick, so he stayed home. That afternoon, Ruth Meyer heard him fall in the bathroom, so she called his doctor. The doctor rushed over and gave Einstein some morphine, and that alleviated his pain and helped him fall asleep. But the doctor knew that Einstein's aneurysm had started to rupture."

I hoped I was painting a picture for Eddie, so he could join me in "believing." "The next morning," I continued, "a group of doctors arrived at Einstein's house and examined him. They recommended surgery and also told him that the aorta was probably too far gone to be salvaged. So Einstein refused the surgery—"

"There's a famous quote from that day, right?" Good. Eddie was along for the ride. "But I can't remember it."

There *was* a quote, and I dug deep into my memories to salvage it before it was crushed by new memories. "It is tasteless to prolong life artificially. I have done my share, it is time to go. I will do it elegantly."

"Nice. Do you remember the names of his doctors, the ones who came to his house?"

"Dr. Harvey and Dr. Dean. Dean was the doctor who begged Einstein to go to the hospital, but Einstein refused."

"But he ended up in the hospital anyway."

"Meyer called an ambulance." I pictured her worried face. "She couldn't just watch him die at home. She was devoted to him. She'd been taking care of him for decades." I filled in another detail. "She spent a lot of time by his side at the hospital during those last two days."

I pictured her stationed outside Einstein's room, shooing away unwanted guests and reporters, just as she'd done for him when he'd been healthy. I saw her conferring with Dr. Dean, then I saw Dr. Dean giving Einstein sedatives.

The scientist was in pain.

I saw Einstein wake up in his hospital bed on the last day of his life and ask the nurse, Mrs. Ander, for pen and paper. He wanted to write something down, something that he wouldn't let die with him.

I watched him write out his deathbed confession, his secret, and with that final image in my head, I was ready to go to the Caves. There, I'd go through Einstein's last days again. Hopefully, I'd still remember them.

*

As we walked across campus toward Grace Hall, my regrets about not telling Laura the entire story started to grow. I should've warned her. But there was no way to convince her that time travel was real without showing her, and that would've most definitely sucked her into the vortex.

I told myself that the best protection for her would be to fix this. That argument sounded cowardly, but it was logical. To a point.

We entered Grace Hall, went down to the basement, and headed into the Caves. We moved through the tunnels without saying a word. I was thinking about Einstein's final days, cycling through the details again, hoping not to forget them.

We arrived at Alex's carrel. I unlocked the door and stepped inside—

A gunshot rang out, echoing through the tunnel.

I immediately ducked to the ground, then whipped back around to shut the door, when another shot rang out and Eddie went down. I crawled forward and grabbed him, suppressing my visceral reaction to the gaping wound in his head, and dragged him all the way into the carrel as two more shots rang out, kicking up sparks from the tunnel walls.

I slammed the door shut, locked it, and went back to Eddie. Part of his temple had been blown off, leaving ragged flesh in its place. Blood burbled from the wound, thick and endless, and his mouth was moving slightly.

There was a kick at the door, then another.

"Ch... change it... back." Eddie rasped.

A gunshot thumped the door.

I thought about getting Eddie to a hospital, but that was a pipe dream. His face had gone totally pale and he was gasping for air.

Someone, and I'm sure it was Van Doran, kicked at the door, then shot at the lock.

I looked from Eddie to the stone wall.

Eddie's hand moved toward his pocket. "J-Jacob." His whisper was hoarse, with barely any life to it.

I leaned down, and Eddie took a deep breath. The blood was thicker now, and darker. His chest tightened as he braced himself for his final words.

"Y-you've been—p-planning to visit Einstein in—P-Princeton Hospital for twelve years... You just didn't—know it."

Exactly. That gave me the boost of confidence I needed. But when his last breath passed and his eyes went blank, I almost lost that boost. His life was now in my hands.

Three more shots hit the lock, then Van Doran kicked at the door.

I looked down to see what Eddie had been reaching for. He'd been pulling out the fifties cash from his pocket. I took it, buried my fears and doubts, and stood up to face the bare stone wall. It was time for me to resurrect Eddie.

I pictured Einstein in that hospital bed, writing down his final words, and I ran as fast as I could into the wall.

Chapter Twenty

The white ocean engulfed me, the temperature rose, and I felt sweat beading on my forehead. I kept running. The oxygen started to vanish, and I gasped for air, running until there no longer was any. Then overwhelmed by the heat of a flameless fire, I stumbled to the floor, welcoming its cold surface.

The white ocean slowly dissipated, and the familiar cracked, cement slab of Weldon's basement floor came into focus.

I rose up on one knee and took deep, measured breaths. After a couple of minutes where Eddie's death weighed heavy on me, I regrouped and headed to the staircase. My plan was to get through the house as fast as possible and check the date only if it was safe to do so. But that wasn't critical. I could find out the date at the drive-in.

I headed up the stairs, wondering if the Dorothy Theorem had worked. If it hadn't, then I'd never be able to resurrect Eddie, much less the old history.

I cracked open the basement door and peered into the kitchen. Late afternoon sunlight was streaming through the windows, and I hoped it was the sunlight of April 17, 1955—or close to it. Einstein had died on the morning of the eighteenth at 1:18 a.m.

My view of the kitchen was severely limited, so it was possible someone could be on the other side of the door. But after a minute or so of silence, I decided the coast was clear, opened the door, and stepped through.

The kitchen was pretty much the way it'd been the first time I'd arrived in the fifties. That was a good sign, but it didn't mean this was April 1955, or that I'd arrived in the right history, the one where Einstein had died in the hospital.

I rushed toward the hallway, but just before I entered it, I heard footsteps. They were moving quickly.

I hung back in the kitchen and heard Clavin say, "Yes, Mr. Weldon."

Part of me wanted to run back into the basement and wait till the coast was clear, while another part wanted to see if I could glean some information.

The curious part won out.

I knew the study was down the hallway, so Clavin had probably stepped into it to talk to Weldon. I peered into the hallway and saw light spilling out from the study.

Without hesitation, I moved down the hallway, just enough to eavesdrop and still have a cushion for a quick getaway.

"How long has Professor Einstein been in the hospital?" That was Clavin.

"Two days. He sounded very ill, Henry. He barely had the strength to talk."

Both men went silent for a few seconds, as if they were acknowledging the gravity of the situation. That gave me the time to calculate that if Einstein had been in the hospital for two days, it was the seventeenth. My timing had been perfect. Einstein would die late tonight. But I'd have to rush to Princeton.

Weldon spoke up, again. "Albert said he'd leave a note should he take a turn for the worse."

The note, the confession, the secret?

"Do you think he discovered something more about the bridge?" Clavin asked.

"That's what he implied."

"Have you told Mr. Van Doran?"

"I couldn't. Greg went through again," Weldon said, and more silence followed, giving me the distinct impression that Weldon wasn't pleased with Van Doran's wanderings. "Albert may die, and if he has an insight into how time travel works and it dies with him, I'd never forgive myself." I heard the sound of shuffling papers. "I want you to drive to Princeton and be ready in case Albert doesn't recover and leaves that note."

"I understand, sir. I'll call you when I get there."

That was my cue to leave. I'd have to race Clavin to Princeton, so I started right then.

I hurried back down the hall, took the connecting hallway into the dining room, and raced through the foyer and out the front door. I sprinted along the front of the house, circled around the large garage, ducked into the woods, then headed to the back of the property.

As I moved through the woods, I replayed the conversation I'd just heard. It explained, finally, the anomalies in the appointment books that Meyer had kept. It was now clear why she didn't note how long the meetings with Clavin were going to be and why Einstein had no appointments for the next two or three days: because Einstein *hadn't* been meeting with Clavin. Those weren't appointment times Meyer had been noting. They were the times Clavin was set to arrive in Princeton to pick up Einstein and chauffeur him to Cumberland. And Einstein had no appointment afterwards because he'd stay there for the next two or three days. Henry Clavin worked for Weldon and *that* was his connection to Einstein.

I also thought I now understood how Weldon and Van Doran were connected. Weldon, who'd discovered the portal while at UVA, had confided in Van Doran about his precious discovery, and Van Doran had brought in Einstein.

When I made it to the road, it was almost dusk. I trudged forward, parallel to the road, under the cover of the forest. Cars roared by, probably heading to the drive-in. When I approached its perimeter, I saw that proved true. The parking lot was half-full, but filling up fast. Tonight's feature presentation was *To Catch A Thief,* which made sense, considering what I was about to do.

My plan for the drive-in was fairly basic, because it took into account my experience as a car thief—which was none. I'd buy a walk-in ticket, then stroll toward the concession, checking out the back row of cars, on the lookout for one that was currently empty of driver and passengers.

Once I spotted my mark, I'd meander over by the driver's side, as if I were headed toward the front of the drive-in, and check to see if the keys were in the ignition. If they were, I'd make my move. If not, I'd repeat the process. The car had to be in the last row, so I could back it out easily and head directly for the exit.

*

The cars were ten deep at the ticket window, and as I walked past them, my thoughts went to my dad. I hoped he wasn't working tonight. I didn't want to face him.

By now, he'd have seen that I'd never published the promised news article. He'd know that I'd taken advantage of him, and somewhere in the back of my mind, I feared this disappointment had been a terrible blow to him and had affected the rest of his life.

At the ticket window, I waited for the car in front of me to pay then bought my ticket using a bill from Eddie's cash. I silently thanked Eddie for his final gesture. If he hadn't reached for his pocket, I would've forgotten the cash from the fifties.

Inside, a few employees, all teenagers, were guiding cars into rows. Maybe the younger kids weren't working this evening because it was a school night. Still, I was on the lookout for my dad.

I casually headed over to the concession stand, and as I did, I scanned the parked cars. There were very few cars along the back row because spots were still available closer to the screen. And those that were there all had someone inside.

While standing in the concession stand line, I began to scout cars in other rows. Specifically, cars parked at the end of a row, so they weren't blocked in. But from where I stood, I couldn't tell if the passengers were in those cars or not.

As the concession line moved forward, more cars rolled into the drive-in, and I watched them, hoping some would opt for the back row.

None did.

Then I found myself at the front of line, ordering a burger. That wasn't part of the plan, but it beat loitering around, looking suspicious.

I stood to the side of the concession stand, ate my burger—which was unexpectedly delicious, rich with flavor, like a gourmet burger rather than a fast-food burger—and watched more cars park. As I finished the last bite of my burger, a short unspooled on the big screen.

No Hunting, starring Donald Duck.

The back row of cars was proving to be a bust, so I sauntered down toward the front, checking each row as I passed. Some patrons *had* set up lawn chairs in front of their cars, leaving their cars empty. But even if they had left their keys in the ignition, they were parked too far into their rows to allow for a quick getaway. Just as I wasn't a car thief, I wasn't a stunt driver. I needed a clear path out.

I was about halfway down the lot when I heard car doors slamming behind me and quickly turned back to check it out.

A car had just parked at the end of a row that I'd passed. Two kids, around six and ten, were hurrying to the front of the car. Their mom joined them, while their dad headed to the back of the car. He opened the trunk, and a few seconds later, slammed it shut. He came around the car, carrying lawn chairs, then unfolded them and headed toward the concession stand. The kids and their mom sat down and starting watching Donald Duck.

I was already moving back toward their car, plotting my getaway. The route from their parking spot to the exit looked fairly clean. And there were no cars directly behind their car, which gave me plenty of room to back their car out, swing it around into the lane, and race to the back. Near the concession stand, I'd have to hang a left.

My hope was that I'd be closing in on the exit before a major uproar about the stolen car had started. Even if the family and nearby patrons were already yelling about the thief, the commotion would take a minute to make its way to the back.

I was about ten yards away from the car when I saw him. *Richie*. He was walking in my direction, but I couldn't tell if he recognized me.

I thought I could make it to the car before he got there, so I didn't change my course. Not with the family engaged with

Donald Duck and the car sitting empty right there at the end of the row. This was too good an opportunity to pass up.

Richie and I moved closer to each other, and my eyes fell to his shiny plastic nametag, *Richie Morgan*, as if I had to verify, again, that he was my dad.

I avoided making eye contact with him. Instead, I glanced at the kids and their mom in their lawn chairs as I walked by them. The kids didn't as much as breathe in my direction, they were so riveted to Donald Duck, but the mom smiled at me. I returned the smile, moved on to the car, and glanced down into the driver's side window—

The keys were dangling from the ignition.

My heart started to pound.

There was no excuse now, except for Richie. I glanced at him before reaching down for the car door handle—and he was staring right at me.

"Hey, mister. What happened to the article?"

"It's not ready yet. I'm sorry." That was abrupt, but I knew that if I wavered in the least, I wouldn't go through with this.

I opened the car door, slid inside, and shut the door as gently as possible so as not to attract the mom's attention. I reached for the ignition, and hesitated—exactly what I didn't want to do.

My wildly beating heart moved into my throat. It was now or never. Time to ignore my fear and use my adrenaline rush, which was flooding my body and telling me to run, to turn the key.

I did, and the car roared to life with so much muscle that it startled me. This powerful behemoth was a far different breed than the fuel-efficient, compact car of the future.

The mom and kids looked back toward the car.

I jammed the gearshift from park to reverse, looked back over my shoulder, and backed the behemoth up.

Then I jammed the gearshift forward, and lurched headlong, tires squealing, into an arc that put me into the lane heading toward the concession stand.

A couple of people with popcorn and sodas in hand were walking toward me, and I was ready to swerve around them, when they kindly obliged and scooted out of my way.

As I bore down toward the concession stand, I could see the faces of the patrons in line, including the dad's face, in shock. Everyone scattered, realizing they were in the path of a crazed car thief.

Except for the dad. He stood his ground.

Was he going to try and stop me?

I was gaining speed, so the dad had about ten seconds to decide whether to make a heroic stand or get out of the way. I had the same amount of time to decide whether to start my left turn early to avoid him, a turn that would be so sharp from here that I'd surely wipe out.

It was a classic game of chicken—and the dad caved in.

He jumped out of the way, and I made my left turn a few seconds later, but it was still too sharp and the car wiped out, skidding to a stop right in front of the concession stand.

I pressed on the gas and the car jerked forward and was back up to warp speed in no time, hurtling toward the gate.

But it wasn't really in no time. Unfortunately, it was just enough time for Richie to come running out from the interior of the back row, waving his hands and yelling for me to stop.

What happened next, happened in a flash. There was no time to slow down or swerve or avoid the inevitable.

I saw the front of my behemoth of a car slam into my own dad, the kid with the bluest eyes ever, who loved films more than anything, and heard a sickening, bone-crushing, *thud.* He disappeared from sight almost as quickly as he'd appeared.

The car continued to hurtle forward, and while my mind went into hyper-drive, my body went into autopilot and continued to execute my disastrous plan.

It was too late to stop. The damage was done.

Nausea filled my gut and my limbs were trembling.

I'd killed my father. That was for sure. No way had he survived that blow.

The car plowed forward toward the exit, and in its wake, I heard the screams of horrified people.

Chapter Twenty-One

I gripped the steering wheel hard, as if it were the only thing keeping my thoughts from spinning out of control. My entire body was pulsing with queasiness and dread. My nightmare had reached the proportions of Greek tragedy.

Time travel was messy, but how could I have killed my own father? If this were a science-fiction tale, I would've disappeared right about now. Without a father, I couldn't have been born. But this wasn't a science-fiction tale. It was fact. Time travel wasn't like it was portrayed in the movies.

As a wave of nausea swept through me, my car roared down the road toward Cumberland. I considered stopping to puke, but if I stopped, it would turn into a permanent stop. The magnitude of what I'd just done would paralyze me.

I had to keep going because *I had to fix this.* More than ever. *Einstein's confession is the key.*

I clung to that. Otherwise, there would be no salvation.

I thought about Dorothy's Theorem. Belief had worked. It had transported me to the right time. But doubt still crept into my thoughts. Sure, I had evidence that belief dictated the workings of wormholes. But that wasn't evidence that Einstein's confession could bring my dad back to life.

That seemed more like faith.

I muted the doubt and tried to concentrate on the task at hand. Regardless of my belief, regardless of faith or not, I had no other option but to move forward.

The road in front of me was dark and lined with thick woods. In the distance were headlights, but it was too soon for the police to be headed this way, and there were no flashing red lights up ahead.

How fast did law enforcement respond to a crime in the fifties? Probably way slower than law enforcement in the future. Still, when it came to the heinous crime of running over a child, it wouldn't be moving at a snail's pace.

The speedometer said I was doing fifty, so I pushed the car to sixty, and pulled the directions out of my pocket. The first turn would come up when I hit Cumberland proper. Take a right onto Mechanic Street, which led to 68 East, which led to 220 North. Then came a thirty-mile stretch of flat-out driving.

Within minutes, the lights of Cumberland shone through the thinning woods. Over the next few miles, I debated whether to abandon this car or not. How long would it take before the police started to hunt it down?

Luck favored me in one way. When I hit 220 North, I'd be in Pennsylvania, which meant there'd be some jurisdictional issues between the local and state police of Maryland and those of Pennsylvania, not to mention good old communication problems.

I hit the lights of Cumberland, and it was then that a new concern crossed my mind. Was there evidence of my monstrous act festooned on the grille of the car? I was cruising through a quiet residential neighborhood, with no traffic, so I weighed whether to pull over and check. It was a Sunday night and my guess was that everyone was either inside the picturesque homes lining the street, sitting in front of their boxy TV sets, or they were at the drive-in.

A car turned onto the street and headed my way. As it passed, the driver, a middle-aged man with glasses, looked over, tipped his hat, and smiled. I smiled back, and was reminded that luck favored me in another way, too. The fifties were a less-suspicious time.

I decided not to pull over and check the car. That would be the more suspicious move. Instead, I kept my eyes peeled for Mechanic Street. The half a dozen other drivers that I passed all looked at me and nodded. I nodded back to all of them.

I turned left onto Mechanic Street, drove through another residential neighborhood, and stuck with my decision. There'd be no pulling over to check the grille, or to switch cars.

Within three minutes, I'd merged onto Route 68, and a few miles later, I was gliding down the open road of Route 220, crossing the border into Pennsylvania. There were a couple of cars behind me and none in front of me. It was obvious that in this decade, people didn't rush around at all hours.

As for me, I was barreling through the night at sixty-five miles an hour, the posted speed limit. I could've gone faster, but I didn't want to hand myself over to the police.

It wasn't long before the steady, full hum of the engine and the stillness of the night led me back to the image of Richie's face. How it had suddenly appeared right there in front of me, terrified, followed by a hard, sickening thud, before it disappeared in a rapid jerk beneath the long hood of the car.

His parents probably knew by now. They were devastated. I'd killed their boy. They would live the rest of their lives with a hole in their hearts, forever grieving. I wished I'd been erased from existence, like would've happened in the science-fiction version of time travel.

I glanced down at the gas gauge and forced myself to make some practical calculations. The tank was three-quarters full. Estimating the size of the gas tank, the poor gas mileage of the fifties, and the number of miles I had to go, I'd have to fill the gas tank once to cover the round trip to Princeton.

If I topped it off now, I'd have to get gas another time, too, on the way back from Princeton, in the wee hours of the morning, should I be so lucky as to have accomplished my mission.

Gas would wait. I'd roll the dice and run down this tank, aiming to stop only once for gas.

I sped up, exited Route 220, and followed my directions for getting onto Route 76, the Pennsylvania Turnpike. Once there, I began the two-hundred-and-twenty-mile sprint that would take me to within thirty minutes of Princeton.

There were very few cars on the turnpike, so I upped my speed again. The sooner I arrived by Einstein's bedside, the better chance I had of getting to that confession before Einstein handed it over to Clavin.

As the miles started to pass, the turnpike lulled me into a comatose state, which was a good thing. I didn't want to see my dad's blue eyes and I didn't want to hear that sickening thud. There were long stretches of total darkness. Gloomy, undeveloped hinterlands, interrupted only by lit interchanges and a few pairs of headlights.

As I closed in on Princeton, I saw a sign for an upcoming service plaza and snapped out of my daze. This was an opportunity to gas up now, instead of waiting for the return trip. If the gas station was still open.

A few miles later, I pulled into that plaza. It boasted a Howard Johnson's restaurant and an Esso gas station, both open. The parking lot had three cars in it.

I drove toward the gas pumps, but when the gas pump attendant stepped out of the cashier's booth, I instantly changed course and swung the car around into the restaurant parking lot. I'd forgotten that this was an era when gas attendants pumped your gas, cleaned your windshields, and checked your tires.

The bottom line was that I needed to check my front grille for signs of my crime before allowing anyone near my car. I pulled into a space far from the three cars in the lot and out of view of the large bay window that fronted the restaurant.

Before stepping out, that feeling of dread came over me again. Would I find blood and flesh on the front grille? Well, it didn't matter, did it? I had to get the job done regardless. I turned to the back seat in search of something to wipe the front of the car with. There was something there all right, but using it seemed callous and creepy.

On the back seat was a small, pink, button-up sweater. It must've belonged to the young girl I'd last seen riveted to Donald Duck. Her life would now always be tied to the death of that child at the drive-in. Her family car was the weapon that'd killed him.

I checked the glove compartment, hoping there'd be a handkerchief or a stack of paper napkins tucked inside. There wasn't.

I grabbed the pink sweater and stepped out into the chilly night. As I moved around to the front of the car, I scanned the side of it to make it look like I was one of those obsessive car owners constantly checking for dings. This was my feeble attempt to cover up my true purpose in case the gas attendant or a restaurant patron was watching.

Not really wanting to face the grille, but also knowing I couldn't delay the inevitable, I looked down at the front of the car. My eyes ticked over the grille from right to left and stopped on some small, bloodied scraps of clothes, lodged between the metal slats.

I lunged at them with the pink sweater, and as I did, I noticed there was something stuck to the inside edge of the oversized bumper.

A chunk of tattered flesh.

Turning away from the horrid sight, I knelt down and freed the scraps of bloodied clothes from the grille, using the sweater. Some stuck to the sweater and some fell to the ground.

When the slats were free of evidence of the crime, I forced myself to look back at the globule of flesh, then scraped it off the bumper, keeping it all wrapped in the sweater.

Then I reached down and collected the pieces of clothes that had fallen to the ground. Just as I was finishing up, I noticed something stuck farther back into the slats of the grille.

I reached in with my free hand and wedged it out. It was my father's plastic nametag.

Richie Morgan.

My mind went numb for a second, no thoughts. Just a flood of darkness, like the thick gloom I'd been driving through all night.

I stuck the nametag in my pocket.

Then, from my kneeling position, I checked the grille, the bumper, and the ground, making sure all the grisly evidence was gone.

It was.

The only evidence that remained was the grille itself. It was ever-so-slightly curved inward at the point of impact. But the bumper was unscathed. Cars of the fifties were tanks.

I stood up and scanned the parking lot for a trashcan, then thought better of it. It'd be smarter to put the sweater in the car, drive back into the hinterlands of the turnpike, pull over, and bury it in the woods. I walked around the other side of the car, scanning every inch as if I were still on the lookout for dings, made my way around the trunk, stopping to buff a spot with my shirt sleeve, then ducked back into the car and stashed the sweater under the passenger seat.

Rather than drive off as if I had something to hide, I went straight for the Esso station. At this point, I thought it'd be less suspicious to get the gas and be done with it. The attendant probably wasn't thinking that this guy is a child murderer. At worst, he was thinking that this guy is an odd duck.

As soon as I pulled up to the pump, the attendant was at my window, offering to *fill 'er up and check the oil.* I said yes to the gas and no thanks to the oil check. He went to work, gassing up the car and cleaning my windshield and windows.

I paid him with Eddie's cash and told him to keep the change. He gave me an enthusiastic *good night, sir,* and I pulled out and onto the highway. My goal was to get rid of the pink sweater as soon as I entered another long stretch of country darkness.

As soon as that stretch came up, I couldn't pull over fast enough. My emergency flashers stayed off. I didn't want to attract the aid of a Good Samaritan, or worse, a policeman. But I did flick on the interior light.

I inspected the floor for evidence, retrieved the sweater from under the seat, checked the floor again, then clicked the interior light off and got out of the car.

The forest was bathed in a haunting glow, courtesy of the pale gibbous moon. I trudged through the underbrush, and about twenty yards in, knelt down and brushed the leaves away from the dirt. With my hands, I dug out a two-foot-square shallow grave.

I laid the sweater in the tiny grave and covered it with dirt.

The temptation to say a few words was strong. A prayer or a couple of lines of tribute to Richie Morgan, the kid who loved movies. But I didn't give in to the temptation. That would've meant giving in to this current history. Accepting its facts.

I couldn't do that. I had to ignore the power of this moment. Only then could I resurrect the flesh that I'd just buried. Only then could I breathe life back into the set of facts that made up the only history that mattered.

I quickly spread the leaves back over the grave, then stood up, ready to take off, when I suddenly remembered that there was one more piece of evidence I needed to bury.

My dad's nametag. It now felt heavy in my pocket. I pulled it out and knelt back down. But I couldn't do it. Something was telling me not to bury it. Even though I wasn't superstitious, I had this feeling that the nametag had been embedded in the grille for a reason.

I stuck it back into my pocket and hurried to the car, hoping my hunch was right. If it turned out to be wrong, and the police tracked me down, the nametag would link me directly to the crime.

Chapter Twenty-Two

The rest of the trip was uneventful. It consisted of the dead of night, the engine's drone, and the headlights of oncoming cars, which were few and far between.

I pulled off the turnpike and navigated the final streets to Princeton. When I arrived, the town was fast asleep. On my way to the hospital, I saw less than a half dozen cars on the road. Every store was shuttered for the night and every house was a dark silhouette.

The hospital was a different story. Though not every room in the five-story building was lit, quite a few were, including some on the third floor, home to the hospital's most celebrated patient.

I pulled into the parking lot. Two dozen cars were clustered close to the hospital, but the rest of the lot was empty. I didn't want to look conspicuous, so I parked near the cluster, but left myself a clean escape route. I checked the time on the car clock.

History had recorded that Einstein had already been sedated and would die in an hour. It had also recorded that he would mumble something in German first. But what history had not recorded was what Clavin had told me during his own deathbed confession.

He told me to take it, to give it to Mr. Van Doran.

According to Clavin's final words, Einstein would hand his confession to Clavin and ask him to deliver it to Van Doran. I hadn't thought about it before, but one deathbed confession was shedding light on another. Time travel was messy, but it had an elegant side to it.

By now, Einstein had probably written down his secret, and it was sitting next to his hospital bed. Of course, it was also possible that Clavin had already come and gone, with the secret in hand.

As I entered the hospital, I was on the lookout for him. The lobby, including the visitor waiting area, was empty, except for a security guard seated behind a broad desk. In modern times, the pending death of a major icon would've filled the lobby with reporters clamoring for updates and gossip. There would've also been a police presence keeping order.

I had to pass the guard to get to the elevators. He eyed me as I did, forced a smile and nodded. I nodded back and added a casual "Hi."

"Howdy," he said, keeping his eyes on me.

I walked by a line of phone booths, stepped up to the elevators, and pushed the "up" button.

"Excuse me, sir. We don't allow visitors after nine o'clock."

Luckily, I was ready for this. I knew that Einstein had been allowed visitors at all hours, and that these visitors were either family members, like his son, who'd flown in from San Francisco, or close friends, like a mathematician whom Einstein had known for over two decades.

I walked over to the guard. "I'm Professor Stanton and I'm here to see Professor Einstein," I said. "I drove down from Harvard as soon as I heard he wanted to see me."

The guard looked me over, and I hoped that when he got to my oversized pants and shoes, he'd peg me as a nerd, and that this would fit in with his vision of a professor.

I glanced around the lobby, leaned in close to the guard, and lowered my voice to just above a whisper. "Professor Einstein and I are working on a secret project."

The guard's eyes widened, and he scooted his chair up to his desk and closer to me. "I think he's doing okay," he said. "He's had some other visitors up there." He nodded to the elevators. "Third floor. ICU. Room 314."

"Thanks," I said, and quickly walked back to the elevator. It arrived, and as soon as the door closed, I braced myself for what lay ahead.

I stepped out onto the third floor and into a long sterile hallway. The nurses' station was at the far end of the hallway, but it was presently nurseless. In the other direction, three people stood outside a room, which was about two thirds of the way down the hallway.

Without a doubt, that room was Einstein's.

As I walked in that direction, my legs began to feel as heavy as lead and my thoughts became a jumbled tangle of things that could go wrong and had gone wrong.

This wasn't the time to let panic take over. To escape my thicket of thoughts, I fixated on my surroundings, glancing inside rooms as I passed them. Patients were hooked up to IVs and bulky monitoring equipment. A nurse was in one of the rooms, administering oxygen to an elderly woman.

Then I turned my attention to the three people standing outside Einstein's room. They were already watching me. But so what? What did I expect? I met their stares with a half-smile, indicating that they had nothing to fear from me, and logged their identities.

Ruth Meyer, Einstein's assistant. Hans Albert, Einstein's son. And Alfred Frank, an economist and Einstein's good friend.

No sign of Clavin.

Getting past Hans and Alfred wouldn't be too tough, but Meyer would be a different story. Not only was she always protective of Einstein, but she also knew every one of his friends, acquaintances, and colleagues. I couldn't claim to be someone Einstein knew, so I planned on telling her I was a reporter for the *New York Times*, on standby, in case Einstein wanted to issue a statement.

The trio was standing on the other side of the doorway, so I peeked into Einstein's room as I passed. He was lying motionless in his hospital bed, eyes shut, his face gaunt and pale. A nurse was checking one of his IVs. *Mrs. Ander, the nurse who'd hear Einstein's final words.*

As soon as I looked back at the trio, I met Meyer's stern stare and threw my original plan out the window. I nodded and continued past her, as if I were going to another room.

I walked past two closed doors and weighed my next move. After two more closed doors, I came to an open one, and stepped inside.

An overweight man in his fifties was fast asleep in his hospital bed. He was connected to a few pieces of bulky monitoring equipment. Their green lights colored the otherwise dark room with an eerie patina.

I stood there, just inside the door, like a phantom in this poor man's life. And I hoped to stay right there for the next few minutes because my new plan was to wait Meyer out.

History had recorded that she hadn't been at Einstein's bedside when he'd died. And considering he'd die within the next hour, that meant she was on her way out. Same with Hans. He was staying with his dad, and since Meyer lived in Einstein's house, he'd leave with her. Alfred would be the first to go because Meyer would make sure all visitors were gone before she took off.

But what about Clavin? With Meyer standing guard, how would he get the confession? And what if he did get it, while I stood here waiting? To come so close to discovering the secret, literally within a few yards, and then have Clavin glide right by me, with the treasure in hand, would be so tragic as to be comical.

And with that thought came a new insight. A wrinkle I'd never considered before and one that gave rise to a new plan, the best of the night.

I'd always assumed that Meyer had known Clavin. But that was before I'd discovered that Clavin worked for Weldon, and that his connection to Einstein was basically that of a chauffeur who drove the scientist to and from Cumberland.

At the same time, I'd always been sure that Einstein had never told Meyer, nor anyone, his secret, which I now knew meant he'd never told her, nor anyone, about the wormhole and Cumberland.

So it was likely that Einstein had never introduced her to Clavin. To her, he was just a name in an appointment book.

Armed with that insight, I was no longer going to wait Meyer out. My new plan was to go into Einstein's room now, rather than risk losing the confession to Clavin.

And I was just about to step out of the room when the overweight man opened his eyes. I hoped he wouldn't spot me, the phantom in the green light.

But he looked right at me. I expected to see fear in his eyes.

I didn't. Instead, I saw pale-colored eyes, green or blue, eyes that were questioning me. Was he having a hard time processing who I was?

"You're g-gonna be him," he said.

A cold chill swept through me. How could this man know what I was going to do? Was he somehow outside of history, aware of the trails?

I waited for him to say more. But as he stared at me with his blue-green eyes, I realized that *I* was the man outside of history, and somehow he'd spotted that. He kept his eyes on me, and I was suddenly fearful that if he told me one more thing he shouldn't know, my tenuous understanding of my new reality would collapse like a house of cards.

I quickly turned, stepped out into the hallway, and was relieved to see that Meyer, Hans, and Alfred were gone. I wouldn't even have to implement my new plan. I headed toward Einstein's room with a little more confidence. My quest for the confession might finally come to an end.

The door to Einstein's room was open, and I walked right in only to stop dead in my tracks—

Meyer was by Einstein's bedside, and it was too late to turn around. I had no choice but to put my plan into action. At least Hans had already left.

"I'm sorry to intrude, but I thought the professor was alone." I stuck out my hand to shake. "I'm Henry Clavin."

Meyer regarded me for a few seconds, warily, and I wondered if I'd blundered. Surely she'd noticed that I'd entered another room just a few minutes ago.

She finally gave me a very light handshake. "The mysterious Mr. Clavin makes an appearance," she said. "I'm Miss Meyer."

I gave a small bow of acknowledgement. Under the circumstances, smiling was inappropriate, but I was pleased that something had gone my way.

"And may I ask what business you have with Professor Einstein?" she said.

"He asked me to come. He had something to give me. I'm sorry I wasn't able to get here sooner."

"Why did you go into that other patient's room, Mr. Clavin?" She was on the ball and to the point.

"I didn't want the others who were with you to know I'd come to see Professor Einstein."

"And why is that?"

"Those would be the wishes of the professor."

Her stern face relaxed. I'd said the right thing. She knew that Einstein wanted his work with Clavin to remain private.

With this small triumph under my belt, I looked over at Einstein. Up close, I could see how much he'd declined since our brief encounter at the Weldon estate. His face was skeletal and his eyes, though closed, were sunken.

Then I glanced at the table next to his bed, checking for the handwritten notes. There weren't any papers on the table. I wondered if Clavin had already come and gone.

"Professor Einstein had not told me you were coming," Meyer said.

I didn't want to risk rocking the boat—now that the boat was in smooth water—with a response that would put her back on guard. So I didn't respond at all and waited for her to take the lead.

She did. "Perhaps you could tell me what you and the professor were working on, Mr. Clavin. Then I might be able to locate what he wanted to give you."

That was way more forward of her than I had expected, but who could blame her? She wanted to know about the man who'd been meeting in secret with her beloved employer.

"If I said any more, I'd be betraying Professor Einstein's trust," I said. "I know he has few secrets from you, Miss Meyer, but telling you about this project would put you in danger." And that was truer than she'd ever know.

With great sorrow on her face, and love, she looked at Einstein. She had worked for this man for nearly thirty years. "Then you'll have to return tomorrow to talk to the professor, Mr. Clavin."

There would be no tomorrow.

So where was that confession?

Meyer started toward the door, expecting me to follow her out.

I had no choice but to comply.

But just as she was about to step out of the room, an accented voice, feeble and thin, said, "May I have paper and pen."

We both turned to Einstein. His eyes were rheumy and searching the room. Meyer instantly hurried toward him.

"Of course. Would you like me to prop you up?" she said.

"Yes."

As she grabbed two pillows sitting on a chair, I scooted out of Einstein's angle of vision and weighed whether to duck out of the room.

If I stayed, I'd actually witness Einstein writing down his secret. But if Einstein saw me, he could give away the whole game. All he had to do was ask who I was and Meyer would know that I wasn't Clavin.

Meyer brought the pillows to Einstein and helped him lean up. By the time she'd placed the pillows behind him, I was out of the room. I hoped I hadn't cut it too close and that the scientist hadn't caught a glimpse of me.

Outside, I stood to the side of the door and peered back into the room.

Meyer was pulling a sheaf of paper from the drawer of the table next to Einstein's bed. She riffled through the first few sheets—which, according to history, had equations scrawled on them—and peeled them off.

Then she pulled a magazine from the drawer, used it to back the remaining sheets of paper, and handed the bundle, along with a pen, to Einstein.

He started writing, and I stood there, flabbergasted. I was watching the great scientist writing the very confession that I'd been seeking for twelve years. After all the extraordinary things I'd experienced over the past few days, this was the most amazing.

In the silence, as Einstein wrote, I wondered where Clavin was, and for the first time, considered the possibility that Clavin's memory had been faulty. *Maybe Einstein* doesn't *hand him the confession.* Maybe Clavin had been too sick that day in Rockville to remember that he'd come for it, but had never gotten it.

I looked over at Ruth Meyer, who was patiently standing by Einstein's side as she had for nearly thirty years. Could Einstein have given her the confession?

"I should not have waited," Einstein said, as he continued to write. "Please deliver this to Henry Clavin or Gregory Van Doran."

Just then I saw Nurse Ander step out of a room down the hall. History had recorded what was going to happen now. I had no doubt that she'd go into Einstein's room to witness that he was writing *words*, and not equations.

And that's exactly what she did.

She walked by me, we exchanged smiles, and then she entered the room and approached the scientist.

That's when I heard the elevator door open, looked down the hallway, and saw something that plunged me right back into the messiness of time travel—

Alex was stepping out of the elevator. He was wearing hospital scrubs.

Chapter Twenty-Three

What the hell was going on? And with that question came the obvious answer.

Alex is here for the same reason I am. The confession.

And he must've come here before Van Doran murdered him in the hit-and-run.

When I looked back into the room, Meyer was heading toward me. She stepped out of the room, glanced at the man in hospital scrubs heading our way, and apparently thought nothing of it.

"We'll wait until he finishes the letter," she said. "Then I'll tell him that you're here to take it."

Nurse Ander stepped out of the room, writing something on a chart. I thought she might call Alex out as an impostor, but she walked right by him, her nose in that chart, and said nothing.

Alex stepped up to Meyer and me. He ignored me and spoke to her. "I'm Dr. Mason, and you must be Miss Meyer. Dr. Wiseman asked me to check on Mr. Einstein."

"Thank you, doctor," she said.

Alex glanced at me, blankly, as if he didn't know me, then headed into the room.

Meyer, the worry now back on her face, turned to me. "Excuse me, Mr. Clavin. I'd like to see what the doctor has to say." She stepped back into the room.

Was Alex going to get to the confession before I did? Had that been his end game from the start? I couldn't very well move into the room and fight him for the confession. Not with Meyer here. Or could I?

Alex suddenly stepped out of the room. "Hold tight," he said.

"Do you have it?" I responded.

"No."

Over his shoulder, I saw that Einstein was saying something to Meyer.

"I have to play this right this time," Alex said.

"This time?" I asked, but didn't need an answer, because I suddenly understood it all. He'd tried to get the confession many times and had failed. So he'd recruited others to help him. Unsuspecting others, like me.

I shoved him against the wall. "You wasted twelve years of my life!"

"But it wasn't a waste. It gave you a purpose."

"That should've been my choice."

"It was. You could have stopped at any time. But you didn't want to."

"Why'd you drag me into it?"

"Because it always plays out the same. The specifics change, but not the outcome. The confession gets lost in history, *every time*. I needed to change that. I needed help." He looked at his watch. "I'll show you what I mean."

He started down the hall, but I hung back, not wanting the confession to walk out of Einstein's room in someone else's hand.

"Don't worry, you aren't going to miss your opportunity. Not yet, anyway."

I didn't move.

"Like it or not, we're on the same team now," he said. "We both want to see those pages."

I followed Alex down the hall and into the room with the overweight man and the eerie green patina. I wondered how many times Alex had ducked into this room and if that was why this patient had turned prophetic.

Alex ignored the man and walked up to the window. "See, it's playing out just the way it did last time... and the time before that... and the time before that..."

I stepped up to the window and saw a car pull into the parking lot and park. Van Doran stepped out and started toward the hospital.

"He's here for the confession?" I said.

"Like he always is, and I always stop him."

"*You* get the confession?"

"No. I never end up with it."

"Then who does?"

He grinned.

"*I* do?"

"That's up to you," he said, and headed back across the room.

"What do you mean?"

"Time travel is messy."

"Thanks for the insight. Why is up to me?"

"Because you've made it this far."

That wasn't a good enough answer. He stepped out into the hallway and I followed. "Alex—*you* don't make it this far. Van Doran kills you in the original history."

"What makes you think that's the original history?"

I realized I didn't know.

"It may become the history of record, but it hasn't yet," he said. "The only way to save the old history, to save Eddie, yourself, and even Einstein, is to get that confession."

"Einstein's confession is the key."

"Always has been." The elevator doors slid open and Alex stepped on.

"Where are you going?"

"To stop Van Doran. But I don't know how much time I can buy you."

I had one question left. "If I can't get the confession, does Laura die, too?"

"Yeah."

"Because of me?"

He nodded. "Fix this now. Once and forever."

The elevator doors slid shut.

I hurried toward Einstein's room, then slowed to a walk before entering. Meyer was standing next to Einstein's bed, her back to me and her head slightly bowed, in a pose of silent grief.

My first thought was that Einstein had died. There'd been no final words to Nurse Ander in German. Meyer had been the last person to see Einstein alive, which would have been a more fitting end.

But then I realized that the monitoring equipment was still displaying Einstein's vital signs.

I approached Meyer, and she turned to me. She was holding two sheets of paper, folded once over. The rest of the sheaf of papers was on the table, next to the slumbering Einstein.

"He's finished with his letter, Mr. Clavin," she said, but she didn't hand me the letter, and I knew better than to reach for it.

This old-world woman, Einstein's protector, would hand me the letter when she was ready to. "How do I know this is for you?"

I hoped Einstein had said something. After all, he'd told Weldon he might leave something in writing. I needed an answer, and got one. It came from the original history. From Clavin himself on his own deathbed in Rockville, more than sixty years from now.

"I'm to deliver it to Mr. Gregory Van Doran," I said.

"That's right," she said, and I saw the relief on her face. She was doing the right thing.

She turned back to Einstein, and while clutching the letter close to her body, gazed down at him as if she still wanted his blessing to hand me the confession.

As I waited for that blessing, I thought about the biggest mystery of the night. *Why wasn't Clavin here to pick up the confession?* And why hadn't I asked Alex about that?

Meyer turned back and offered me the letter. "Good luck, Mr. Clavin."

As I reached out and took the letter, my heart started to race. Triumph, disbelief, and fear all coursed through my veins at hyperspeed. After twelve years, I held the Holy Grail in my hands.

"Thank you," I said, after way too long a pause. I was ready to race out of the room, but forced myself to act properly. "I'm sorry about the professor's health."

"Thank you."

"Goodnight, Miss Meyer."

She forced a sad smile, and turned back to Einstein.

Chapter Twenty-Four

I stepped out of the room and hurried down the hallway, past the empty nurses' station, and toward the stairwell. Taking the elevators was too risky without knowing where Alex and Van Doran *and* Clavin were.

In the stairwell, I was tempted to stop and read the confession, but I plowed ahead, down the stairs. Getting as far away as possible from Van Doran was the first order of business.

The stairs ended on the first floor at a large metal door marked *Exit To Parking Lot*. Perfect. I pushed down the door handle, ready to complete the first lap of my escape, but it didn't budge.

I pushed again. The door was locked for the night. It'd be decades before fire codes would force such doors to remain unlocked.

I swung around in the other direction, moved out of the stairwell, and into a hallway of administrative offices.

The hallway ended in a set of double doors, and based on where I was in the building, I was pretty sure that the lobby was on the other side of those doors. Every step in that direction came with a stronger urge to read the confession.

I resisted the temptation by folding the two pages and stuffing them into my pants pocket, next to my father's nametag.

I pushed through the double doors and found myself in the lobby. The security guard was gone and I wondered if he'd been drawn into the battle between Van Doran and Alex. I wouldn't be wondering long.

Outside, I ran toward the parking lot, turned the corner of the building and was body-blocked hard by a big man. The blow left me sprawled on the asphalt.

I looked up to see Van Doran standing over me, his gun trained on my face. "Give me the confession."

"Why? You're going to kill me anyway."

"You're right. But if you give it to me, you get to know what it says before you die."

And I buy myself some time, I thought. "Where's Alex?"

"He didn't survive."

"But he said he always stops you."

"Looks like 'always' was too strong a word. Now give me the confession and we both get to learn how to control the chaos of time travel."

I was out of options, out of time. I breathed in deeply, hesitated, then finally reached into my pocket and slowly pulled out the folded papers.

Van Doran, now wearing a smug grin, leaned down eagerly to grab it—

And I jammed the pin from my dad's nametag into the palm of his hand.

He jerked back, and in that instant I rolled into his legs, and he went down. I pounced on him and landed three quick blows to his head, and two more to his midsection. Then I scooped up his gun and the confession and ran to my car.

Without looking back, I jumped inside, keyed the ignition, and pulled out of the lot.

Ten blocks later, I pulled into an alleyway between two shops, ready to give in to my curiosity and read the confession before I lost it again.

I unfolded it, and my mouth went dry. I was stunned.

The sheets were blank.

Meyer hadn't given me the confession.

Clavin ends up with the confession. Like he always does.

Without hesitation, I pulled out of the alleyway, drove right back to the hospital, parked, and hurried to the hospital. I didn't see any sign of Van Doran, but I didn't look too hard. My goal was to intercept Clavin.

Inside, the security guard was back at the counter. I passed right by him, not wanting to be slowed by small talk, glanced at the line of phone booths, and *that* slowed me down—

Clavin was inside the middle booth, on the phone.

Was he on his way up to get the confession or on his way out *with* the confession? It was impossible to know, and before I could even debate my next move, the elevator doors and Meyer stepped out.

As soon as she saw me, her eyes widened with fear.

"Please, Miss Meyer," I said. "Tell me who has the letter."

She hurried past me.

I went after her. "Miss Meyer! Did you give it to someone else?"

She stopped in front of the security guard and announced, "This man should not be allowed upstairs." The security guard eyed me.

"Please tell me who has it?" I pleaded.

"That letter was not meant for you," she said. The fear in her eyes had been replaced by anger in her voice. "Professor Einstein saw you in his room, and you are not Henry Clavin."

"Does Mr. Clavin have it?"

"That is none of your business."

With that, she turned away and marched toward the exit.

The security guard stood up from his desk and put his hand on his holstered gun, daring me to go after her. "Let's give the lady a few minutes to leave the lot," he said.

I weighed whether to ignore his warning, and glanced at the clock above the elevators—Einstein would die in three minutes. That information suddenly gave me another critical insight.

The night is playing out exactly as it should. As it had in the original history. Meyer wouldn't be by Einstein's side when he died and that meant Clavin already had the confession. She'd given it to him. It had to play out that way because Einstein fell back asleep after writing his secret down and he'd awaken just one more time, any minute now, to say his final words in German to Nurse Ander.

I looked back at Clavin. He was still on the phone.

"You can leave now," the guard said.

"Okay," I replied, but didn't move. It was critical I stay with Clavin.

"Visiting hours are over, sir."

"I understand."

Clavin finally stepped out of the phone booth, so I started toward the exit, hoping he was headed in that direction, too. Glancing back, I saw the guard sit back down, and also saw that my wish had been granted: Clavin was headed out.

I stepped outside, headed to the parking lot, and waited for Clavin to arrive.

When he turned the corner, I approached him. "Mr. Clavin."

"Yes," he said, but didn't stop.

"Can I speak to you for a second?"

"How do you know who I am?"

"I'll explain, but first, I want to talk to you about the note Professor Einstein asked you to deliver."

"You must be mistaken." He was calm and collected.

"I understand the need for privacy, but please hear me out before you leave."

This time he didn't respond. He stepped up to his car.

"I know that the professor has asked you to give the note to Gregory Van Doran."

He glanced back at me with narrowed eyes, either curious or suspicious, then unlocked his car door.

"Mr. Clavin," I said, "I know about the time-travel bridge."

He wheeled back around. The color had drained from his face, and so had the calm veneer. He was afraid. Either of me, or of the fact that someone outside of Weldon's inner circle had discovered their secret.

I was about to blurt out that everything was going to hell and that Einstein's confession was the only thing that could fix that, when Clavin suddenly opened his car door and jumped inside. I grabbed the door handle before he could lock himself in.

As we had a tug-of-war over the door, I quickly weighed my two options. Pull out Van Doran's gun and take the confession by force, or try reason. I went with reason first, using what I'd gleaned earlier in the night—Clavin's hint of distrust toward Van Doran.

"You've seen Van Doran many times at the Weldon estate," I said. "You know what kind of man he is. Professor Einstein doesn't. If he did, he wouldn't be entrusting him with that note."

The tug-of-war over the door lessened.

"I don't know what that note says," I continued, "but I'm only asking you do to one thing. Read it and decide. *You* decide if it should be delivered to Van Doran."

Clavin was no longer pulling on the door.

I stopped, too. "If that note explains the rules of time travel, or if that notes explains more about how the bridge works—do you want Van Doran to have it?"

Clavin looked past me, toward the hospital. He was weighing whether to talk to Einstein, but I knew that he'd dismiss that. He worked for Harold Weldon. It was his employer who'd be the final arbiter.

"I'll show it to Mr. Weldon first. Before I show it to Mr. Van Doran."

"You should. But please read it now, yourself, before you leave."

"Why?"

"Because you may never get to show it to Mr. Weldon. Van Doran will try and stop you."

Clavin shifted uneasily in his seat. His eyes widened a bit, as if he were imagining that exact scenario and it made him uncomfortable.

But he didn't pull out the confession.

He needed one more nudge to put him over.

"You're part of this, Mr. Clavin, whether you want to be or not. Mr. Weldon trusted you to be part of it. Read that note now, and if there's nothing to fear, I'll be on my way, and you'll be on yours."

Clavin pulled the confession from his pocket. It consisted of one piece of paper. He unfolded it and read it as I stood there. I didn't as much as breathe. I didn't want to stop the momentum.

I looked up to the third floor of the hospital. Right about now, Nurse Ander was listening to Einstein speak those few words in German. In another minute or two, he'd die.

When I looked back at Clavin, his forehead was creased with worry and his shoulders were sagging. There was no doubt that the confession contained something critical.

Clavin finished reading, looked up at me, then back down at the note.

Finally, he handed it to me. "Read it," he said, in a somber voice.

I did.

It was addressed to Van Doran, and Einstein started right in with his concern about *the bridge,* his term for the wormhole. The confession was built around a brilliant analogy and there was no introduction, preamble, or ramp-up.

Dear Professor Van Doran,

I have concluded that time travel is like a virus on the face of human history. And history can only survive if that virus is eradicated. So far, the virus has done little damage. You've not traveled enough through the bridge to impact the powerful momentum of current history.

But if you or anyone continues to travel, it is as if you are spreading the virus. And if the virus multiplies, the history of humanity will change.

Please do not misunderstand what I am saying. When we consider all the horrors that our history has produced, a new history may be an improvement. But as long as we don't know how to control the effects of time travel, we are doing nothing more than spreading the virus.

God may not roll dice with the universe, but we are rolling dice with the history of humanity. The outcome may

be even more tragic than the history we have inherited.
I've run through countless mathematical proofs and I've
concluded that we could bring an end to humanity itself.

Therefore, these travels should not continue. There is too
much that is unknown. We don't have the theoretical tools
to understand how the bridge works, or the practical tools
to use it wisely.

You must eradicate the bridge, and you must do it now,
for if our secret ever made it out into the wider world, it
would surely be exploited. The bridge is too much of a
temptation to those who wouldn't be troubled by the serious
consequences of using it.

Harold may not want to destroy that which he has
discovered, but you must, for certainly you understand the
danger. To close the bridge, you must make it collapse on
itself. To do this requires a sudden burst of energy, a
controlled explosion, at the mouth of one of the entrances. I
ask you to carry this out as my time on this earth is over
and I cannot.

> *Yours very truly,*
> *Albert Einstein*

This wasn't what I'd expected, but it validated everything I'd
learned up to this point. *Time travel is messy.* But Einstein's
confession went way beyond that. Time travel was too complicated
to comprehend; and, therefore, too risky to use.

Time travel is dangerous. That was his conclusion. It was so
dangerous that we shouldn't be using it. *At all.*

I handed the note back to Clavin. "Van Doran has traveled
many more times than Einstein could've ever imagined."

"The professor would be shocked if he knew how many times.
But how do *you* know?"

"Because I'm one of the results of the virus."

But I was also the cure.

I realized that history was playing out as it always had, though with these bizarre undercurrents that were never recorded. I could've never interpreted the facts and come up with the details and motivations that I'd witnessed and participated in. No interpretation of history would have led me to the truth of what I was now living.

I was helping history to play out as it had. As it *should*.

But for this version of history to remain intact, Einstein's final wish had to be granted.

"I'm going to close that bridge tonight," I said.

"I have to show the note to Mr. Weldon," Clavin said. He had to take his cue from Weldon. That was his job.

But it wasn't mine. "I understand. But please call him and tell him what it says."

Clavin didn't respond. He folded the note and put it back in his pocket. Maybe he didn't want to tell his boss he'd read the note in advance, which I'm sure wasn't proper protocol.

I didn't wait for a response. "Good luck," I said, and headed to my car, ready to go back to Cumberland. I wouldn't count on Clavin or Weldon to fulfill Einstein's wishes. I'd do it myself.

My bet was that Van Doran was headed back to Cumberland, or possibly Charlottesville, depending on which side of the bridge he needed to enter. By now he'd have decided that he'd come back to earlier tonight and try again to nab that confession.

And he was right to try again. According to Einstein, it was more than possible to change history completely, and Van Doran was so very close to doing that. He'd murdered Einstein, Alex, Eddie, Clavin—and that had given the new history its powerful momentum.

There was only one thing left that stood in Van Doran's way. Me. The old history, the real history, was counting on that. That's why it had delivered Einstein's secret into my hands. The confession had always been the key. *But only if someone acted on it.* Van Doran hadn't been able to wipe it out, and as long as it existed, I had a chance. History had a chance. Einstein, Alex, Eddie, Laura and Clavin had a chance to live out their normal lives. But I had a strong feeling that the next time Van Doran came back to this night, he'd succeed in destroying the confession—and there would be no more chances.

I had to stop him.

Chapter Twenty-Five

Fifteen minutes later, I was on the Pennsylvania Turnpike, headed back to Cumberland. There was even less traffic than before and the darkness was thicker. So thick that it looked like I was on the road to nowhere. The lyrics to "Bohemian Rhapsody" reverberated through my head.

Is this the real life? Is this just fantasy? Caught in a landslide, no escape from reality?

I was caught in a vortex and there was only one way of escape. Sealing the wormhole. I hoped that Clavin had called Weldon and told him what the note said. But even if he had, I couldn't be sure how Weldon would react.

My thoughts then turned to detonating an explosion to seal the wormhole. Again, my skills weren't suited to the task at hand. For example, my first thought was dynamite, as if I were Wile E. Coyote battling the Road Runner.

Eventually I hit on the idea of using the natural gas from Weldon's kitchen stove. I could use a hose to run the gas into the basement. But if you were aiming for an uncontrolled explosion, that was it. And I'd have to get through the wormhole first before igniting the gas.

I also considered sealing the wormhole from the Charlottesville side, after I went through. That came with its own set of problems. If the Dorothy Theorem worked, and I returned to the right time—the start of the fall semester, with me as an adjunct professor—it'd be tough to gather bomb-making materials without arousing suspicion. And even if I managed to pull that off and detonated the explosion, the entire university would go on high alert for a possible terrorist attack. SWAT teams would swarm the campus, followed by the FBI and Homeland Security, and they'd ultimately get their man. Me.

One of the service plazas was fast approaching, so I turned to a more immediate problem. Getting another car. I'd hit Cumberland after dawn, and in the light of day, the Cumberland Police would have no trouble spotting the car that had killed a defenseless child.

I slowed down as I advanced on the plaza. The restaurant and the gas station were closed and the parking lot was empty. If I wanted another car, I'd have to pull off the turnpike and scour the streets of whatever small town I found myself in. And that's what I planned to do.

Meanwhile, I focused on my own history. I had to keep it alive because I'd soon need it for the Dorothy Theorem. I concentrated on the day I'd headed to the faculty orientation in Charlottesville. The day I'd met Eddie. The day I'd met Laura. I wanted to return before Eddie had taken me down to the Caves and sucked me into the vortex. Before I'd gotten fired. I needed to feel the excitement of starting my new job again. The excitement of that fresh start.

It worked. I got lost in that world, and before I knew it, I noticed the dark of night had given way to the ghostly light before dawn. I was now close enough to Cumberland to change cars.

I pulled off at the next exit and entered the small town of Plattville. The main streets of the tiny downtown were still fairly empty at that hour. There were a few delivery trucks doing their rounds, and I considered stealing one, but rejected that idea. A truck would be too unwieldy.

The edge of town gave way to a used-car lot, a miniature golf course, and some restaurants, all shuttered for the night. Then I made it to a residential neighborhood with blocks of single-family homes. I parked my car at the end of one block, got out, and walked down the street, checking all the cars parked along the curb. No one had been kind enough to leave keys in the ignition.

I walked down three more blocks, but came up empty-handed. Maybe the delivery truck was the best option after all. I turned around and headed back toward my car, but using a different route so I could peer into another set of cars. Still no luck.

As I headed back to the turnpike, with the thought that I'd try one more town, a larger one, before entering Cumberland, I passed the used-car lot and an image suddenly popped into my head. I'm sure it came from thousands of hours of media consumption. It was an image that'd been replayed so many times on so many TV shows that it was probably part of the collective unconscious.

A block past the used-car lot, I parked, got out of my car, and walked back to the lot. If that image was going to pay off, there was no need to check all the cars. Either my sudden inspiration was the policy at this car lot or it wasn't.

There were four cars right next to the entrance. I stepped up to the closest one and reached for the door. It opened. I bent down and flipped over the floor mat. Sure enough, there were the car keys.

I slid into the car, keyed the ignition, and drove off the lot.

By the time someone reported this crime, I'd be gone from the fifties. Hopefully. I checked the gas gauge and found I was good on that front.

Back on the turnpike, I calculated that I was less than an hour away from the Weldon estate. If I went with the plan to use natural gas for the explosion, I still had to stop for matches and materials for making a fuse so I could delay igniting the gas until I'd gone through the wormhole.

My exit came up quickly, and soon I was speeding down Route 220, then Route 68 into Cumberland. Early-morning commuters had finally joined me on the road, and seeing them repopulate the world convinced me to put the kibosh on stopping again for anything. I'd look for matches and fuse-making materials at the Weldon estate.

As I drove through Cumberland, more traffic began to fill the streets, including a police cruiser approaching from the other direction. There was no doubt that the officers inside would check me out as they passed. Not only did passing drivers in the fifties acknowledge each other, but also these officers would be on the lookout for the drive-in killer.

As the cruiser passed, the officers looked right at me. Was the fear that rippled through me obvious on my smiling face?

They didn't return my smile.

I checked my side-view mirror and saw their brake lights blink on behind me. They were slowing down.

I was ready to floor it.

But their brake lights blinked off.

I located the cruiser in my rearview mirror, and watched to see if they were going to pull a U-turn.

They didn't, and my fear slowly ebbed away.

I reached the outskirts of Cumberland and braced myself for passing by the drive-in. It was just up ahead. After reading Einstein's confession, I now knew that I'd contributed to the new history by killing my own father. The new history was just as efficient as Van Doran when it came to getting rid of loose ends. And just as brutal.

I glanced back at the rearview mirror, and my heart started thumping at a thousand beats per minute.

There was a police cruiser behind me.

I suspected it was the same one I'd just passed, which meant the officers had recognized me. Probably from a description given by that mom at the drive-in. I white-knuckled the steering wheel so hard that I felt blood pulsing through my hands.

The cruiser didn't have its lights on yet, and I wondered if that meant there was still some doubt in the officers' minds. As I drove by the empty drive-in, I couldn't help but feel that this was where my trip would end.

When I glanced back at the rearview mirror, the cruiser was even closer.

I was ready to floor it and get the hell out of Maryland. I'd head to Charlottesville and travel back to the present from that side.

The cruiser pulled into the drive-in. I looked back over my shoulder, and this time I caught a glimpse of a couple officers and two police cruisers parked on the other side of the concession stand.

I understood what was going on. The police were doing more investigating under the light of day, and the officers behind me were joining them.

My heart was still beating wildly, so I tried to will it to slow down. I needed to think straight. Weldon's estate was coming up and I couldn't just pull over onto the side of the road. Not with the police so close by. If the officers noticed, they'd investigate.

So I drove past the estate, looking for a place to pull over on that side. After a mile or so, I parked the car on the shoulder as close to the woods as I could. The car was still plenty visible, but I didn't want to drive any further in search of better place to hide it. The longer it took to hike back to Weldon's, the more time Van Doran had to wipe out the history I was clinging to.

Before I took off for the mansion, I searched the car for matches or anything else that could help with a makeshift explosion. The glove compartment was empty, but I found a road flare in the trunk. I grabbed it, thinking that it'd be useful as bomb-making material, though I'd have to figure out how.

Twenty minutes later, I was trudging through the woods up to the back of Weldon's house, planning my next move. If Clavin hadn't called Weldon and told him about the note, there was no chance of getting Weldon on my side. And if he wasn't on my side, I couldn't very well go about the business of piping natural gas into the basement.

So my default plan was to subdue Weldon with Van Doran's gun, which I still had, then tie him up and get on with sealing the wormhole.

I opened the French doors, stepped inside, and stood stock-still, listening.

The house was deathly quiet. Unnaturally so.

After a minute or so of that unnerving silence, I made my way through the house, down the hallways, toward the kitchen. I stopped when I saw the light in the study was on. Was Weldon in there, anxiously waiting for Clavin to return from Princeton?

I pulled out Van Doran's gun, ready to rush the study. But inches from the doorway, I put the gun back in my pocket, opting to see first if Clavin had called Weldon.

I stepped into the room. "Mr. Weld—"

Weldon was sprawled out on the floor, his skull bashed in. Blood had already pooled over a wide area of the hardwood floor. The elegant sculpture of the golden tiger lay in the sea of blood.

It wasn't hard to figure out that Clavin *had* told Weldon—and that Weldon had done the right thing. He'd tried to stop Van Doran.

It was time to seal the bridge.

As I hurried to the kitchen to check on the gas stove, I thought of a glitch in my plan. I'd be sealing the bridge with Van Doran on the wrong side of it. I'd have to wait for his return. But I *couldn't* wait. I was sure he'd get the confession this time. And we both couldn't end up with it. Only one history could survive.

And that's when a huge piece of the puzzle suddenly fell into place. A piece of history that I'd forgotten. A fact from the correct history.

History had recorded that Van Doran disappeared right after Einstein's death, and that no one had ever found out what happened to him. *That's because he gets stranded on the other side of the bridge,* if *I can seal it tonight.*

But I had to get through it first.

I stepped into the kitchen and heard a door shut somewhere in the house. Was Van Doran still here? That didn't seem possible. But if he was, I wouldn't allow him to use the wormhole. That was paramount. I went down into the basement.

As I stood there in the dark, a horrible thought dawned on me. *Does Van Doran disappear tonight because I kill him?*

The nausea and dread that I'd felt earlier in the night once more found its way into my soul. This man had gone rampaging through history, murdering others, but was I ready to stop him by committing murder myself?

His victims would be resurrected if I fixed everything. Alex would live. Eddie would live. Clavin would live a long life and so would Weldon. But Van Doran would die tonight, murdered at my hands, and he'd stay murdered—or, as history would record it, *disappeared.*

I pulled out my gun and waited in the dark, unsure if I could kill Van Doran in cold blood.

The seconds went by and the house was quiet. Then I heard a scream, a kind of wail, and I knew what had just happened.

I ran out of the basement, through the house, and into the study. Clavin was collapsed on a chair, and tears were sliding down his face.

"We can bring him back to life," I said. "This is another history. It doesn't have to exist."

Clavin didn't say anything for a few seconds. With wet and fearful eyes, he stared at Weldon's lifeless body. Then he looked at me, and a steely cold took over his demeanor. "Tell me what I need to do."

*

Henry Clavin and I didn't use natural gas or my pilfered road flare to execute Einstein's final wish. There were plenty of flammable liquids in the house, so we made small "bombs" by dumping the liquid into four empty paint cans.

We placed those cans into a metal trashcan, which we set up against the basement wall. Then we filled the trashcan with gasoline and created a fuse from rags.

After I was safely through the wormhole, Clavin would use the fuse to ignite the gas, which would heat the paint cans until they exploded.

"There's something I don't understand," he said, after I told him about everything that had transpired because of the bridge.

"How can we really know what the old history—the real history—is?"

"I'm not sure we can," I said, and I wasn't. But from everything I'd seen over the previous few days, and from what Einstein had written, I hoped we could preserve most of that old history. "None of this quite fits together in a way that we'll ever understand."

"That's what worried Professor Einstein."

"Time travel is messy."

Clavin smiled for the first time. "I heard him say that, too. On the last weekend he was here."

"He was right."

With everything set, I had one thing left to do. Focus on that day in August, the day before I'd driven to Rockville and met Henry Clavin for the first time.

I pictured myself rushing across the UVA campus, past pristine lawns, and heading up the steps of Old Cabell Hall. Eddie suddenly approached me and wanted me to skip orientation. He pulled out his copy of *Fame*—

Here, my mind started to wander. Probably because of the gas fumes wafting through the basement. Instead of sticking to that day, I saw my copy of *Fame* magazine in a box of magazines at a yard sale. I saw Alex stepping out of the elevator in hospital scrubs. I saw Van Doran shooting Einstein. I saw my stolen car speeding through the drive-in and smashing into my dad.

My thoughts were too scattered to make a run for the wall.

I saw Clavin and Ruth Meyer at Princeton Hospital, and then I saw the synchronicity of the hospital rooms I'd been in. Clavin's, Laura's, and Einstein's.

Then I latched onto the fleeting image of Laura.

I saw her trekking up Jackson Hill to Gray's Cabin and then I saw her on the day we first met. In the Iliad Bookstore. It was the same day that I hoped to return to. I walked in to pick up the packet of handouts for my class.

Laura didn't look up, but I could still see she was beautiful. She was concentrating on her book, and her short red hair fell over one of her cheeks.

I walked up to the counter.

She looked up, revealing hazel eyes.

I told her what class I was teaching, and her jaw tightened in anger.

She looked me over and then called me the lucky winner.

I joked about Alex, which made her grin.

That night, we hiked up Jackson Hill and looked over the dark valley. We talked about her future and mine.

She was the woman I hoped to get to know during my tenure in Charlottesville.

I ran into the wall and was immediately engulfed in the heat of the white ocean. I ran until the oxygen began to disappear and the whiteness became infinite. I stumbled down and felt the cool stone floor.

The ocean started to dissipate and gave way to the carrel around me—and, more importantly, what was in the carrel.

Alex's desk and bookshelves. *And* his books and files.

I was back.

Chapter Twenty-Six

I made my way through the Caves, up through the trap door, and into Grace Hall. Before I exited the building, I grabbed a campus paper from a stack by the entrance and checked the date.

The Dorothy Theorem had worked. I'd come back to the right day. If all was back to normal, or close to it, Alex would be in New York, and I hadn't yet been fired from my new job.

Outside, I asked a student the time. His answer told me what I had to do next. Talk to Eddie. At this point in the day, Eddie had already approached me with his copy of *Fame*, but he hadn't yet told me about Clavin's resurrection.

My car was exactly where I'd parked it the last time I'd lived through this day. So getting to Eddie was going to be easy. But deciding what to say to him wasn't. My goal was to stop him from researching Einstein's secret any further. I wanted to make sure there was no chance of changing history again.

I could've counted on the wormhole being sealed to stop the changes, but I wasn't ready to. Not yet. I'd count on that only when I was sure the changes had stopped.

As I drove to Eddie's place, I realized that our roles would be reversed. Instead of him trying to convince me to drive up to

Rockville, I had to convince him *not* to. I had to convince him that he'd already done his job. That he'd already talked me into pursuing his lead, and that his lead had paid off.

And there was only one way to prove that.

I knocked on Eddie's door. When he answered, he raised his eyebrows in surprise. "I thought I'd have to do a little more lobbying to get you to help me."

"I'm a sucker when it comes to Einstein's secret."

"Then you've come to the right place." He motioned me inside.

I sat on the couch and asked him the same question he'd asked me the first time around. "Henry Clavin—How much do you know about him?"

He laughed. "That's what I wanted to ask you."

I repressed the overwhelming impulse to jump right into the topic of bridges and wormholes. My twelve-year odyssey was now over and Eddie had played a major role. I badly wanted to describe to him how Einstein's final night had really played out, even if I sounded insane.

But I didn't jump into it. It was only when Eddie invited me to the Caves, where he said he had something to show me, that I started to open up.

"Clavin didn't die in a car accident," I said.

"You already know?"

"You're the one who told me."

Eddie cocked his head. "What?"

"In another version of history, you took me to the Caves and you told me about Clavin."

Eddie leaned back in the easy chair and stared at me, wide-eyed, as if he were facing an alien, which in a way he was. He was silent for a full thirty seconds before he spoke again. In a quiet, almost reverential tone, he said, "What do you mean another history?"

"You're right, Eddie. Einstein's secret is about time travel. What he called a bridge."

"I never told anyone that."

"You told me."

He stood up, and I wasn't sure if he was going to kick me out, so I forged ahead. "I used the bridge. You did, too."

"This is science fiction, right?"

"When *you* told me about time travel, *I* was the one who thought it was science fiction. But you have a theory, don't you? About Einstein and time travel. And your plan is not to tell me about it just yet. First, you want to tell me about Clavin."

"This can't be happening."

"There's another history that plays out. Or, I should say, *almost* plays out. It's a history that would've replaced this one."

"How can I have told you what I believed if I don't remember telling you?"

"I don't have an answer."

"And how is it that you remember the other history?"

"I don't know. But that's what Einstein's secret is all about. Time travel is messy. He couldn't understand how it worked."

Eddie took a deep breath. "So do you have any proof of any of this?"

"History isn't changing anymore." At least, I hoped it wasn't. Because that was my proof. "Clavin isn't in the hospital up in Rockville. He died in that car accident. Like he always did."

Eddie wouldn't have to go to the Caves to check that out. Clavin's obituary would be right there on the Internet, as it'd been when I'd found it so many years ago.

Eddie hurried into his bedroom and returned with his laptop. He sat down and clicked away on his keyboard. Then he looked up, stunned. "The trails are gone."

"Because there's no more time travel," I said, and silently thanked Clavin for sealing the wormhole.

Eddie went back to tapping away on his laptop, probably racing through the Internet verifying that the trails were truly gone. I sat back, relieved and pleased that the changes had stopped.

After another couple of minutes, Eddie let out a sigh. "So I miss out on the adventure of a lifetime."

"It was more of a nightmare than an adventure."

"This bridge—where was it?"

I told him I'd fill him in on everything later. He deserved to know. But for right now, I had a couple of other loose ends to take care of.

In the back of my mind, I hoped that I wouldn't have to fill him in. Ever. Maybe history would correct itself enough to wipe out what Eddie knew about time travel. And what *I* knew about it.

I was afraid that the more I talked about it, and the more I thought about it, the more the other history had a chance of returning. I'd learned that facts were malleable, and I didn't want to risk changing the historical record again.

*

I headed to Greenley's with the intention of running into McKenzie. In the prior version of this day, McKenzie had spotted me at Greenley's with Eddie, and though there was no way to know if that had played a role in my getting fired, I wanted to change that part of my day.

This time, McKenzie and I would have an amiable conversation about my classes. Then I'd wait and see if that fateful phone call from the department still came. *Professor McKenzie would like to set up a meeting with you in the morning.*

The coffee shop was packed, and as I stood in line, I realized just how much I wanted my firing to have been part of the other history. A trail that had blazed through this history. A history where I got to teach at UVA. A history where I'd been given a fresh start.

I ordered my coffee and waited at the counter.

It wasn't long before Professor McKenzie walked in. He got in line without noticing me, but my hunch was that he soon would. Then I'd get the first hint of whether my dismissal belonged in this history or not.

He glanced around the shop, and his eyes fell on me. I smiled. He returned my smile with the same forced smile he'd used when he'd spotted me with Eddie. That was a bad sign. It wasn't Eddie that had motivated his forced smile. It was the fact that he had to deliver bad news.

McKenzie stepped out of line and headed my way. Another bad sign. Last time he hadn't approached me. But this time I was alone. He didn't have to wait until tomorrow to deliver the bad news.

"How are you?" he said.

"Good. Ready for the semester." *Unless you're going to fire me.*

"I'm glad I ran into you. I was going to set up a meeting, but this is much more convenient."

I braced myself.

"Next year the University is launching an Interdisciplinary Initiative," he said, "and the Governing Board wants our department heavily involved."

I nodded, as if I were interested in the Interdisciplinary Initiative, when in reality I was just waiting for him to lower the boom.

"I'd like you to join our meetings with the Physics and Biology Departments," he said.

A huge grin took over my face, and I quickly dialed it down, so it looked more like the reaction of a professional, pleased with a career opportunity, rather than a kid, pleased with a surprise birthday gift.

"We want to develop more interdisciplinary courses with those departments, and that seems like it might be something right up your alley."

"It is, and I'd love to do it."

"Good. I'll have the Assistant Director email you the information. Good luck with your classes." And with that, he was on his way back to stand in line.

"Thanks," I said, but he didn't turn around.

The barista called out my name, and I grabbed my coffee and headed out.

*

As I walked across campus to my next stop, the Iliad, I thought about the Initiative. Had the other history wiped it out? Was that why McKenzie had fired me? He'd looked over the instructors for this semester and thought, *Why did I hire this guy again?*

But with the Initiative alive and well, I was a good fit. With my appointment, McKenzie could keep Alex, his star professor, happy, and he'd found an adjunct well versed in the history of science. An adjunct who'd be willing to devote a lot of time to working on this Initiative.

Now it was up to me to deliver.

I walked into the Iliad and saw Laura behind the counter, immersed in a book. Her short red hair swung down over one of her cheeks, but even with her face partially hidden, her beauty captivated me, as it had the first time I saw her.

"Hi," I said.

Her hazel eyes took me in. I was a stranger, but I wondered if she could sense that this stranger already loved her. "Do I know you?" she said.

That was a shock. She *did* sense something. "I don't think so," I said, hating that I had to start off with a lie. "Wait—we must've met in one of those multi-universes that I'm always reading about."

She smiled. "That's right. Thanks for reminding me." She closed her book. "What can I help you with?"

"I'd like to pick up my class handouts."

"Which class?"

"5055."

Her jaw didn't tighten in anger. This time around, she was able to hide her resentment. "So you're the lucky winner," she said, still choosing the same words, but saying them without hostility.

"What do you mean?" I was sticking to the script, though I knew exactly what she meant.

"You're Alex's friend from college."

"Jacob Morgan."

"I'm Laura," she said.

"How do you know Alex?" I asked.

"I was in the Ph.D. program with him." She stood up and started toward the back of the store. "I'll get your stuff."

So she wasn't going to bring up my villainous act of stealing her job. Unfortunately, there was a downside to that. Our little confrontation had forced us to open up. It had laid the groundwork for our first date.

She returned with the box of handouts and began to ring me up. "Did Alex tell you we have something in common?"

She *was* going to bring it up.

"No," I said.

"I'm a new adjunct, too."

"Really?" I blurted out, and as soon as I did, I knew I'd just summoned the missing hostility.

"You're shocked that UVA would hire a mere store clerk?"

"I'm sure you're no mere store clerk."

"Not anymore."

I smiled. "Congratulations."

"And congratulations to you. Cash or credit?"

I handed her my credit card. She slid it through the card reader and waited for the receipt to print out. Neither of us said anything. The silence was awkward, but not uncomfortable.

The receipt printed, and she handed it to me, along with a pen. I signed it and gave it back to her. "Thanks."

"The department is a stickler for receipts," she said, then opened the box of handouts and put a copy inside.

I picked up the box, ready to head out and call her later, like I had in our previous meet and greet, but then decided that in this history, the right history, I didn't just walk out.

"How about dinner when your shift is done? I mean unless there's a policy against instructors—" That was ridiculous. Why was I bringing up University policy? We were going to have dinner, not a relationship. At least, not yet.

She laughed. "I'll have to consult the instructor handbook. Meanwhile, why don't you come by around six-thirty?"

"Great." I picked up the box and headed out. "See you then."

*

Five weeks later, there was no doubt that we were a couple. And that made it hard for me to hide anything from her. Not that there was anything to hide except for my one secret. But it was a whopper. I wanted to tell her about Einstein, and I no longer feared the trails of the other history. I'd talked to Alex a few times, and he'd thought it was all over, too, though he was vigilant. "You never know," he said.

My opportunity to bring it up to Laura came in late November, on Jackson Hill. If there was a more appropriate place, I couldn't think of one. Laura and I had hiked up for what she thought would be my first introduction to Gray's Cabin.

Inside, she told me the story of Corbin Gray, while I lingered over the *Life* magazine in the display case. It was the original magazine, the one with Dwight D. Eisenhower on the cover. There was no hint of any other history on the cover or anywhere else in the cabin. Still, this place would forever bring me back to the day when I'd nearly gotten Laura killed.

We continued our hike to the peak, where dusk was falling and a few stars were starting to shine. "I have to tell you something," Laura said. "And I know it's going to sound weird."

Not as weird as what I could tell you, I thought.

"Remember when you first came into the Iliad and I asked if we knew each other?" she said.

"Yeah, and I reminded you that we'd met in one of those multi-universes."

This time she didn't smile. She went right on with what she was planning to tell me. "It wasn't some vague feeling. It was strong. Like I'd known you before. A long time ago. And then somehow forgotten about you until you walked into the store. Like we'd been best friends in junior high and then one of us moved away."

She looked at me, and I was close enough to her to see the pleading in her eyes cutting through the dusk. She wanted me to acknowledge that what she was saying, and feeling, was true. That

I'd forgotten, too, and that together we'd be able to solve the mystery.

"I guess we're going to have to go back through our junior high school days with a fine-toothed comb," I said.

"It could be even further back than that. Like elementary school."

Over the previous weeks, we'd already talked a little about our past. We'd grown up in different parts of the country, but her family had moved a few times. She was hanging her hope on the possibility that she'd lived near me for a short while.

At the summit of Jackson, she spread out a blanket, and I opened a bottle of wine. The night soon engulfed us, blending its darkness with the timeless glow from the stars above. That made it easy to slip into a conversation about our childhoods.

We weren't able to find a time and place where our paths had crossed, but hearing more about her life brought me closer to her. Sadly, for her the conversation was a grand disappointment. She was having a hard time accepting the fact that her instincts could be so wrong. She badly wanted to solve the mystery.

So badly that I felt compelled to tell her she was right. That we *had* met before. That her instincts were spot-on.

I wanted to say those things, but I didn't.

Someday, if we stayed together, which I thought we would, I'd have to tell her. But even if she grew to trust me completely, how could she ever believe such a far-fetched story?

"Maybe it's a kind of reverse déjà vu?" she said, toward the end of the night.

"What's that?"

"I'm creating memories that didn't happen based on what's happening now. That sounds ridiculous, right?"

"It sounds just like reverse déjà vu," I said. *And it sounds like reconstructed memories.*

She kissed me. "Well, it's a messy theory right now, but I'll work on it."

She had the messy part right, and I wondered if she'd eventually get the time-travel part right, too. But that wasn't a comforting thought. Maybe her use of the word "messy" was another trail, a subtle one. And maybe her memory of meeting me long ago was also a trail.

If they were, I hoped they wouldn't grow. But if they did, I'd know why. Another wormhole, another bridge, had opened up.

THE END

Printed in Great Britain
by Amazon